Crossing the Railroad

Published by Phaze Books
Also by Marie Rochelle

All the Fixin'

My Deepest Love: Zack

Caught

Loving True

Taken By Storm

A Taste of Love: Richard

Taken by Storm

Closer to You: Lee

Lucky Charms

Cincinnati, Ohio

Crossing the Railroad

A novel of sensual romance by

MARIE ROCHELLE

Cincinnati, Ohio

A Phaze Production
Phaze Books
6470A Glenway Avenue, #109
Cincinnati, OH 45211-5222
Phaze is an imprint of Mundania Press, LLC.

To order additional copies of this book, contact:
books@phaze.com
www.Phaze.com

Cover art © 2008 Debi Lewis
Edited by Amanda Faith

ISBN-13: 978-1-60659-163-5

First Print Edition – May, 2009
Printed in the United States of America

10 9 8 7 6 5 4 3 2 1

Dedication

To Chelle:
I'm so glad your high school dream finally came true.
Marie

Prologue

The woman stood silently in the shadows as she watched the two people inside the bedroom. She couldn't believe after she had practically threatened him to stay away from that slut, he hadn't listened to her. *Why did he want to embarrass her*? She had spent most of her life in love with Bill Richardson. Hell, she had even tricked him into marrying her right after they finished college. When she first laid eyes on him, she couldn't imagine a time that he wouldn't be in her life.

She had stuck with him all through those long, drawn out law school classes and gave up her dream of being an English teacher just to help him study for his dream. Bill actually thought back then she had been doing it for him, but he was wrong. She had set her sights on him the day he gave the speech to the entire student body the second week of school.

Anna Richardson's gray eyes hardened into cold steel as she listened to her husband's rich baritone voice whisper repeatedly how much he loved the mocha-skinned beauty he was having sex with in their bed.

How could he possibly want Danielle Simmons when he was married to her? Sure, she only stayed with him for the past fifteen years because he was one of the most sought after attorneys in Georgia. She had gotten tired of his hands being on her body years ago, but how dare he disgrace her with their housekeeper?

Sure, back in college, she noticed the black women Bill dated when she was setting her sights on him, yet she didn't think much of it. Didn't everyone break out and do different things when they left home? Drink a little more? Experiment with lifestyles they didn't do before while under their parent's roof? However, after a person graduated, all of that stuff fell into the background as their adulthood approached.

She continued to hide in the dark hallway while her husband made love to Danielle. She hated Danielle the second she laid eyes on her. There was just something so sweet and alluring about the younger woman. Why hadn't she stood her ground and fired the housekeeper? She wondered how long this had been going on. Hell, she didn't want Bill any more. Honestly, even before Danielle entered the picture, her husband had been asking for a divorce, but she wasn't going to let him leave her. She wasted the best years of her life for him, and he owed her big time. If she was miserable in their marriage, then she was going to make damn sure he was, too. No, there wasn't going to be an out for her dear old husband.

However, the more she thought about it, the writing was on the wall about her husband's feelings for Danielle. Bill had always found ways to be around Danielle since the first day she started working for them. When she confronted her husband late last year about his eagerness to help their attractive housekeeper, Bill just blew her off. But she wasn't crazy. Her husband was in love with that woman he was now in their bed with. Without a doubt, she knew it was the truth, because Bill never sounded like that on the rare occasions they had sex.

She wanted to be more upset about Bill cheating on her. She wanted to feel the need to run in there and jerk his perfectly tanned body off Danielle's. Truthfully, she didn't give a damn. All she wanted from her husband was the life he accustomed her to.

"I'm not going to let that tramp take away my wealth. It took me years to get here, and I'll do anything to make sure that it doesn't happen," she promised. Anna took one last look at the couple in bed and made her way down the stairs and out the front door.

Chapter One

Bill Richardson collapsed next to the beautiful woman next to him as a moan of ecstasy slipped through his lips. He couldn't believe how quickly he had fallen in love with Danielle, but he didn't want things to end between them. In reality, he only wanted to make them better, and there was only one way to do that. Reaching down at the end of the bed, he covered them with a light sheet and reached for the woman who had made his life better since she walked through the front door.

"I'm going to divorce Anna," he whispered. He kissed the side of Danielle's neck, pulling her sweaty body closer to his damp one.

Danielle snuggled closer and ran her slim fingers through his chest hair. "You know that she'll never let you leave her for me. We just have to enjoy what we have," she said, sadly.

"No," he shouted and then lowered his voice when Danielle flinched in his arms. He never wanted her to be scared of him. He cared about her way too much for that. "I want more than an hour in the afternoon with you. I'm in love with you, and I'm going to marry you," Bill insisted, stroking Danielle's smooth back with his fingers. He loved how silky her skin was. She was everything he wanted in a wife.

"Bill, you're living in a dream world. You've been married to Anna since you graduated from college. You've built a life with her. I know you're attracted to me, but that's it."

He heard the sadness in Danielle's voice, and it tore at his heart. How could she think he wasn't madly in love with her? Anna wasn't a wife to him anymore. All she wanted to do was throw parties and spend his money. Her snappy attitude towards him had gotten old years ago. He was pushing for a divorce every day, and she wasn't having it. Something had to come to an end and soon, because their living arrangements was getting old.

"Don't you want to be my wife?" he questioned.

"Of course, I do," Danielle replied quickly, staring into his eyes. "But we need to be realistic about this and our situation. I'm your housekeeper, and I've a child from a previous marriage. How will your family, friends, and co-workers think about you leaving Anna to be with me and Joy?"

How could Danielle doubt his feelings for her? Hell, he wasn't concerned about what anyone else thought about them being together. He only thought was about if she wanted to be with him and if she was willingly to wait until he made it happen.

"You know that I love Joy like she was my own daughter. She's such a sweet little girl. After I divorce Anna, I want to adopt her legally as soon as we get married," Bill insisted.

Danielle rose up and gawked at him. "Are you serious?" she stammered.

"I'm not playing with you, Danielle Simmons," Bill grinned. "I love you more than *anything* in this world. I'm going to have my lawyer change my will so everything will be left to you and Joy."

Soft fingers pressed against his mouth. "I don't want to hear about that. I'm not thinking about anything happening to you. It would break my heart if you weren't around for our baby."

Baby?

Bill removed Danielle's fingers from his mouth and sat up in the bed. "Are you pregnant?" he whispered, staring into a pair of killer hazel eyes. He honestly believed Danielle's eyes were the first thing he fell in love with when he interviewed her for the job.

"Yes," she replied in a soft voice. "Are you happy about it?"

He was lost for words. How could she think he wouldn't be out of his mind with happiness? "Baby, I'm more than happy about this. You've made me feel like I'm finally going to have the family I deserve," Bill exclaimed, pulling Danielle against his chest.

"I was a little worried," Danielle confessed in a low voice against his heart.

Moving Danielle back a little, he brushed the hair out of her face so he could look down into her gorgeous face. "Why would you be worried?"

Shit, he was the one always troubled Danielle would drop him for a man closer to her own age. God, he would be forty-two in a couple of months, and Danielle was just twenty-five. Why would she want to stay with someone as old as him? To make matters worse, he wasn't going to get any younger.

"You're married and sleeping with your black housekeeper. Why wouldn't I be?"

"Baby, you're more than the housekeeper," he corrected. "You're the woman I'm in love with. How many times do I have to tell you that?" Bill exclaimed. Reaching out, he placed his hand on Danielle's still-flat stomach. "I want to be there for every moment in our child's life."

Danielle placed her fingers over his and smiled. "I want the same thing, but are you sure Anna will let you leave her?"

"Anna isn't going to have a say in anything I do after today. She made her feelings about me clear a long time ago. We haven't been in love for years, and I'm beginning to think she never loved me in the first place," Bill sighed, removing his hand. "We better get dressed. It's almost time for Anna to come home. I don't want you to be here when I talk to her."

Tossing the light sheet off his body, Bill climbed off bed and watched Danielle as she slid out of bed and proceeded to get dressed. "You're so gorgeous. I can't wait until you're my wife."

Fixing her clothes, Danielle came over to him and gave him a quick kiss on the mouth. "Do you know how much I love you?" The sincerity in her words warmed his heart.

"I think I do, because I feel the same way," he smiled, then moved back from the tempting woman in front of him. "You really better go. I need to change the bed and remake it before Anna comes home. I'll call you later after I finish talking with her."

"Are you positive that everything is going to be okay?" Danielle questioned as he walked her to the door.

"Baby, I'm sure Anna won't be pleased, but she's strong. With a nice settlement from me, she'll leave us alone." Bill walked down the steps with Danielle at his side. Pausing by the front door, he gave Danielle one last kiss and opened the door. "Stay home tonight. I'm pretty sure Anna will toss me out, and I'll need a place to stay."

"You're more than welcome to stay with me. Joy knows that we're in love, and she'll love to have you over. She loved it the last time you read her a bedtime story."

Danielle walked out the door and glanced at him over her shoulder. "I love you."

"I love you too, baby," Bill whispered, and then closed the door.

* * * *

Sitting down at her kitchen table, Danielle watched her eight-year-old little girl playing on the floor with her Baby Alive doll. Bill had bought it for her birthday last week, and Joy didn't go anywhere without it.

Sometimes when she looked at her daughter, she saw traces of Joy's father. Chris had loved their little girl from the second she was born. He did everything with her until the day he died. What healthy twenty-eight-year-old male dropped dead from a heart attack driving home from work?

Joy had been five years old when her father died, and her daughter handled it better than her. After Chris' death, she had to find a job, but she hadn't worked in any field for so long that getting a good job was nearly impossible.

For a couple of years, she had worked odd jobs until landing the one at the Richardson's as their housekeeper. The second Bill Richardson opened the door, the attraction sizzled between them, but she ignored it for the longest time.

She never wanted to be labeled the *other* woman, but late one night her car wouldn't start in the pouring rain, and he offered her a ride home. Joy was spending the night with her grandparents, but she wanted to be home just in case her little girl called and wanted to come home earlier.

After Bill had gotten her home safely, she offered him a cup of coffee as a thank you for giving her a ride. He accepted before the words were completely out of her mouth.

She'll never forget how their relationship began. She was at the kitchen cabinet reaching for two coffee cups when Bill wrapped his arms around her waist and started kissing the back of her neck. It turned out to be the best night of her life. She shouldn't think that away, but she couldn't help it.

"Mr. Richardson, we can't do this. You're married, and I work for you," she moaned turning her neck to give him better access.

"I've been separated from Anna for the past five years. She won't sign the divorce papers," Bill whispered as his fingers unbuttoned the front of her white shirt.

"This isn't right."

"Yes, it is," Bill disagreed as his fingers worked on the front clasp of her bra. "We both feel it, and it would be a shame not to act on it."

Danielle flung her head back against Bill's shoulder when the pad of his thumbs played with her swollen nipples. "Please," she panted, brushing her butt across his thick erection.

"Please, what?" his hot breathed whispered in her ear. "Do you want me to stop?" Bill removed his hand off her breast and had them hovering above her throbbing nipples.

Grabbing Bill's hands, Danielle placed them back on her heaving breast. "Please, don't stop," she begged.

"Sweetheart, I plan on loving this beautiful body of yours all night long and well into the morning," Bill promised spinning her back around. He quickly stripped her out of her clothes until the only thing she was wearing was a pair of black high heels.

As she tried to remove them Bill pushed her hand away. "Don't. I've had fantasies about making love to you in those for months."

"Really?" she exclaimed, watching Bill strip until he was a naked as she was.

A light dusting of brown hair covered his body going down to the huge cock that was pointing right at her. "Mr. Richardson, I can tell you're more than ready," Danielle purred, brushing her thumb over the tip.

Bill's erection jerked and swelled even more. She raised shocked eyes to him. "Wow."

"What can I say? He likes you," Bill exclaimed removing her hand. "But if you don't stop touching him, he won't make it much longer."

"Baby, I'm sorry," she apologized, wrapping her arms around his neck and gave him a long wet kiss. "Is that better?"

Growling in the very back of his throat, Bill picked her up and laid her down on the island behind them. "I can't wait until I learn every inch of this brown perfect paradise that you call your body."

Danielle leaned back on her arms and looked up at Bill noticing the heated look in his bluish-green eyes. "We can't make love here. It's too out in the open."

"No, it isn't," he whispered, covering her softer body with his hairy one. "I want to see all of your gorgeousness when I make love to you." Spreading her legs, Bill slipped the tip of his thick erection inside of her.

"Damn, sweetheart, you're so tight," he panted, adding another inch.

She couldn't think as Bill kept going deeper and deeper inside of her wetness until he was balls deep. Sweat dripped from both of their bodies as he thrust in and out of her at a pace she didn't know was possible.

"Danielle, you feel so good. Once isn't going to be enough for me," Bill swore as he wrapped her legs around his waist, increasing his speed even more. The only sounds in the kitchen were the sweat-covered bodies coming together again and again.

* * * *

"Mommy, what's for dinner? Joy asked, cutting into her memory and snapping her mind back to the present.

"How about pork chops?" she suggested, smiling over at her daughter. Joy was such a pleasure to be around. She couldn't ask for a better child. Joy was the kid most

14

parents dreamt about having. She never caused any problems and was always there to help out anyway she could.

"With apple sauce on the side and macaroni and cheese?" her daughter's young voice asked hopefully.

"I think I can do that," Danielle agreed as she got up from the table.

* * * *

Bill was growing more pissed by the minute back at his house. Why was Anna making this so hard for him? He knew she wanted out of the loveless union as much as him, probably more. Yet, she was fighting for it like their marriage was the best thing in the world.

"I'm not giving you a divorce so you can marry that woman. I don't care if you're sleeping with her, but Danielle will *never* be your wife."

"Anna, we aren't a couple anymore," Bill flung back, hoping to break through whatever wall his wife was trying to build up. When would Anna understand that their marriage ended years ago? "I want to move on with my life. Danielle is pregnant, and I want to make a family with her, Joy, and our baby."

"That bitch is pregnant with your child?" Anna yelled, lunging for him. "She isn't taking anything from my child."

Stunned, Bill moved back from the hate shooting from his wife's eyes. "You're pregnant?" Who's the father?" As far as he knew, Anna wasn't dating anymore.

"Honey, you are," she smirked as she ran her hand over her washboard stomach. She was looking at him like the cat that swallowed the canary.

Anna was lying! He hadn't spent a moment in her bed since Danielle came into his life. She was the only woman he was making love to, and Anna knew that.

"Anna, why are you lying to me?" Bill demanded. "We haven't been together for years."

His wife's thin lips kicked up into a nasty sneer. "My dear husband, you honestly don't remember us having sex?"

"No, because it's a lie," he snapped. "I haven't been sexually intimate with you in years. You aren't my type, and you know it. I'm in love with Danielle, and I'm going to divorce you so I can marry her. We have talked about this before. Why are you trying to lie now to hold on to me? I'm not going to fall for this. Why don't you stop now before you dig a hole that you can't get out of?"

"Bill, don't you recall that vivid wet dream you had about two weeks ago?"

No, this can't be happening to him! Shit, this wasn't for real. Falling down into the chair behind him, Bill felt his heart as it dropped to his knees. "I thought I was making love to Danielle," he groaned. "I was sick with a high fever and the flu. You took advantage of me."

"I did no such thing," Anna denied. Her voice practically had a magical sound to it as she came clean about her deceit. "I'm your wife, and I wanted to make love to my handsome husband. There was a time that we couldn't get enough of each other. Sure, we were still in college. But like I said, there was a time. I thought that night was a glance back into our past. "

Bill wasn't paying attention to a word coming out of his wife's mouth. His mind was too focused on Danielle and what her reaction was going to be about this. She was going to be distraught when he told her about this. She was already fragile, but so loving, when it came to him and their relationship. This might be the thing that ended the romance he was trying to build for the two of them.

"I can't stay here. I have to go and tell Danielle about this," he shouted, jumping up from the couch. "God, I hope I don't lose her over this." Bill made a speedy exit to the door before Anna could stop him.

* * * *

"Danielle, please listen to me," Bill begged, reaching for the woman he loved, but she slapped his hands away.

"Don't touch me, you bastard," she cried, brushing the falling tears away with the back of her hands. "I believed your deception. You don't love me. You just wanted to see how it would feel to *fuck* a black woman."

"Stop saying that right now," Bill demanded, wrapping his hands around her arms and giving her a small shake. "I love you and our baby. That's why Anna did this to us. She was scared. She knew I was on my way out of that house. I still want to be with you and only you."

"Anna isn't going to let you go now that she's pregnant," Danielle sighed, slipping out of his arms. He sensed her immediate withdrawal, and it scared the hell out of him.

"She doesn't have any control over me. I'm going to do what I want." Damn it to hell, he wasn't going to lose the love of his life. Not after it took him so many years to find her and these wonderful feelings.

Moving away from him, Danielle opened the front door. "Bill, you need to leave, and please don't come back. I can't afford the stress. I've my daughter and now this baby to think about."

Bill saw that he was fighting a losing battle at the moment. He wasn't going to push her too much tonight, because Danielle was right. He had just tossed a lot at her. She needed time and some rest to process all of the details.

"Okay, I'm going to leave, but I'm not giving up on us. You and Joy will be my family along with the new baby. We're going to get through this. I love you."

Before Danielle could shoot him down, he planted a soft kiss on her mouth. He poured all the love he felt for her into it. Ending it, Bill ran his thumb over her full bottom lip. "Do you love me?" he asked, moving back so he wouldn't crowd her.

"Yes," she answered in a low voice.

"Good. Get some sleep, and we'll talk tomorrow," he promised. Bill turned and left with ways to win back Danielle's trust running around in his head.

* * * *

Later that night, the sound of banging on her front door woke Danielle up out of deep sleep. She flung on her robe and hurried to the door before the loud noise woke up Joy.

Without bothering to look through the peephole, she opened the door and froze. Two police officers were standing in front of her, and the gloomy expression on their faces made her realize instantly the news wasn't going to be good.

"Are you Mrs. Joy Simmons?" the young blond asked her.

"Yes," she answered as a familiar sinking feeling started to set in. This was like a flash of her past when she got the news about Joy's father.

"We have some bad news for you, ma'am," the younger officer continued. "There was a shooting tonight at a local convenient store, and your boyfriend was shot. We found your name listed as his emergency contact in his wallet."

Tears poured down her cheeks as she held onto the doorframe so she wouldn't faint. She shook off the bad feeling. She wasn't going to think the worst. Bill was fine. There wasn't anything wrong with him. "Is he okay?" Bill wouldn't leave her alone like Chris had. No, he promised they would be a family.

"Ma'am, we're so sorry. He was shot during a robbery, and he died instantly," the other officer filled in.

Her knees buckled, and Danielle gripped the door even tighter. "He's gone?" she choked out.

"Mrs. Simmons, are you okay? Do you need for us to call someone for you?" the young blond officer asked, concern in his deep voice.

"No, I don't, and thank you for your kindness," she whispered moving back as the initial shock was wearing in. Bill was dead. He wasn't going to see his baby grow up.

"Thank you for coming by, officers," she whispered, then closed the door before they could offer her help again.

The second the door closed behind her, she collapsed to the floor. "Lord, why did Bill have to die?" Danielle screamed at the top of her lungs as her grief took over. She lost track of time in those early morning hours. She cried until a pair of small arms wrapped around her shaking body.

"Mama, please don't cry. It will be okay. You still have me and the baby. Mr. Richardson wouldn't want you to be upset. He loved us."

Sucking up the last of her tears, Danielle pulled her little girl's body into her lap. "How did you know I was going to have a baby, Joy?"

"I heard you and Mr. Richardson," her daughter replied, playing with the buttons on her robe. "Is Mr. Richardson in heaven with Daddy?"

Kissing the top of her child's head, she hugged Joy closer to her body. "Yes, baby. He's in heaven with your daddy."

"I like that," Joy replied, snuggling closer. "Now Daddy won't be so lonely."

Danielle blinked back a fresh set of tears as she held her beautiful daughter in her arms. Joy was going to make a wonderful older sister when the time came.

"Mama, can we name the baby Dymond if it's a girl?"

"Why Dymond?"

"I had a dream about the baby, and her name was Dymond."

"Okay, if it's a girl that will be her name."

"Mama?" Joy said again.

"Yes, sweetheart?" Danielle answered, closing her eyes. She rested her head against the front door. A single tear slid down her cheek and dropped on her shoulder.

"I'm going to be the best big sister in the world. Plus, when I get older, I'm going to get a good job and take care of all three of us."

"Really?" Danielle whispered as she tried not to break down in front of Joy.

"I promise," Joy swore right before she fell asleep in her lap.

Chapter Two

Twenty years later

The darkness of the alley made it a perfect place for Ridge Webber to hide waiting to ambush him. Logan Scott paused at the entrance and listened for any kind of sounds to give away Ridge's location. He hadn't been a police officer for twenty years not to take his time. The smell of old garage, pee, and a scent he didn't want to think about burned his nose.

For the past two years now, he had been after Ridge for selling stolen guns and drugs to elementary school children. He needed some hard evidence to get this street punk and menace to society put behind bars. However, Ridge was smart and always found a loop-hole to slip through. It was like he was a cat with nine lives. The last time, a rookie had forgotten to read the bastard his rights, and the station had to release him.

"Logan, do you want me to go down to the other end and block him in?" Peggy Williams, his partner, whispered next to him. "I know he's in there. I can feel him staring at us. He has been waiting for us to come to him, and I think we should flush him out."

Glancing to the left, Logan looked down at Peggy. Despite her being five nine and a half, he still towered over her with his six foot five inches. She had been his partner for about six weeks now since his long time partner Marcus Jackson was assigned to desk duty. Ridge had shot Marcus about eight weeks ago in the arm while fleeing from a scene. He had gone into hiding the same day, and now was the first time in weeks they had him cornered.

"Do you want me to stay here while you go around to the other side?" Peggy asked him, repeating her question. He had to admit, Peggy was fearless. Nothing seemed to scare the woman next to him. Maybe it came from both of her parents being in the military, or she could just have ice water running through her veins. He didn't care which one it was. He was just pleased he hadn't gotten placed with a rookie.

"I think it would be best if I stayed here, and you went to over near the trash cans. I want to make sure he can't have easy access to this street. You know once he gets on the sidewalk, he can blend in with the crowd so easily," Logan complained.

"Okay, give me a chance to get to the other side before you call him out. You know how much he hates to be confronted. He has a quick temper and doesn't have a problem shooting a cop." Peggy eased around him and hurried to the other side of the alley.

Logan waited until he saw her before he called out. "Ridge, I know you're in there. Why don't you come out? Don't make this any harder on yourself. You shot a cop, so you're already in deep trouble. Why are you trying to make it harder?"

"Shut the fuck up," Ridge yelled back from somewhere in the darken alley. "He had it coming, and I would shoot him again without thinking twice about it."

Logan held his temper as Ridge's harsh words pissed him off. He couldn't let this thug get to him. He had to be the one in control. "Why can't you show your face? Or are you too scared to do it?"

"I'm not scared of shit," Ridge yelled as he suddenly appeared a few inches in front of Logan from behind several pilled-up boxes. "How many times do I have to tell the cops I'm not going to jail?" he asked, pulling a gun out from behind his jacket.

He didn't flinch as Ridge pointed the gun at him. Years of training had his emotions under tight restraint. "Drop the gun. I'm not going to let you take me in. I want out of here, and you're going to let me go, aren't you Officer Scott?" Ridge taunted as he aimed his gun for the middle of Logan's chest.

"You don't have any power to make any demands on me. So, why don't you drop the gun? I know you honestly don't want to shoot me today," Logan tossed back as he tried to get through to Ridge. He wasn't positive if Ridge was on drugs or not. It was so hard to tell with him, because most of the time Ridge was just a nasty SOB.

"I don't care about dying. However, can you say the same thing about your pretty partner?" Ridge asked.

A deep line etched across Logan's forehead as he stared at Ridge as his threatening words set in. *What in the hell was Ridge talking about? Peggy wasn't going to die.* "Once again, stop with the empty threats, and drop you gun," he demanded.

"I never make an empty threat, do I Luther?" Ridge moved out a few inches, and Logan was momentarily stunned to see Ridge's partner with a knife up to Peggy's throat. *How in the hell had that happened?* Luther must have been hiding further back in the alley and came up behind Peggy. He couldn't let Ridge know how much this had thrown him. He had to get Peggy away from Luther without him hurting her.

"Luther, let go of my partner, or I'll be forced to shoot Ridge," Logan threatened.

"Don't listen to him Luther," Ridge yelled back at his friend. "Officer Scott isn't going to do a thing. He doesn't want another partner hurt on his watch. Now, why don't you get more comfortable with Officer Williams? I think we might be here a while."

"I can do that," Luther's raspy voice carried through the alley way back to Logan. He could hear the threat in younger man's voice and without a doubt in his mind, Logan knew Luther would kill Peggy.

"So Officer Scott, I think we have the upper hand now. How about you drop that gun and toss it over here to me?" Ridge suggested. "I know you want me really bad, but not at the life of your partner."

Shaking his head, Logan aimed the gun for the middle of Ridge's chest. "I can't do that, and you know it." He had to find a way to outsmart this guy. Ridge was young, but there wasn't anything dumb about him. He had been on the streets most of his life.

"I wish you had listened to me," Ridge said before he fired a shot.

Logan tried to move, but Ridge was a master at firearms, and the bullet hit him in the upper part of his shoulder knocking him to the ground. The burning pain raced through his body. He was able to fire off a shot, but it missed its mark as Ridge raced away from him towards Luther and Office Williams. He saw Peggy fall to the ground as Luther get go of her and raced off behind Ridge. He was trying to stay focused as Peggy hurried over to him.

"Logan, just stay with me," she screamed applying pressure to his wound. "I just called in the shot on the radio. Help is on its way." He noticed the blood make its way down Peggy's neck from the small cut on the side. It looked like a flesh wound, but he couldn't be too sure.

"I'm sorry I didn't know Luther was here with him. I should have known Luther would be with him since he got bailed out of jail last week," Logan mumbled as his started to feel lightheaded. His shoulder felt like it was on fire.

"It's not your fault. Ridge and Luther are very dangerous. I wouldn't doubt if they didn't set this up to get us out here."

"Yes, it was, and I promise not to put you in that kind of situation again." He was trying his best to keep his eyes open, but they were getting so heavy. He just needed to close them for a few minutes. "Tell Marcus what happened and that I'm not giving up on getting Ridge a cell next to his father," Logan mumbled before he closed his eyes.

Chapter Three

The cool gentle touch of fingers brushing a strand of hair off his forehead woke Logan up. Opening his eyes, he stared into a pair of the warmest brown eyes that he had ever seen. They seemed to instantly relax all the tension in his body. He couldn't wait to find out who this woman was.

"Officer Scott, I'm so glad that you're awake. We were getting worried about you. You lost a lot of blood from that shoulder wound," the nurse said, fixing the sheet across his chest.

Reaching out, he placed his hands on top of her dark brown one. "Please, call me Logan," he choked out because of his dry throat.

"Okay," the nurse smiled patting his hand. "I'm Nurse Simmons, but you can call me Joy. I'm the head nurse over you while you're here in the hospital."

He couldn't get over how attractive his nurse was. He wasn't usually fond of hospitals, but it came with his job. However, Joy might make his stay more enjoyable. He had always had a fondness for African-American women. "How long have I been here?" he asked, wincing as a pain shot through his shoulder.

"Three days. Your partner was here an hour ago to check on you. She was really worried."

"I'm surprised that she isn't still here." Peggy was constantly worried about him. Sometimes she acted more like a girlfriend than his partner.

"She was going to stay, but she got a phone call and had to leave. I had to tell her it was against hospital policy to use her cell phone in your room," Joy said as she fixed his pillow. "Do you want me to move your bed up any higher?"

"No, I'm fine," Logan answered, rubbing his head. "Has someone named Marcus been here to see me?"

"Yes, he went down to the cafeteria to get some coffee, and he's coming right back. I'll let him know that you're awake." Joy turned to leave, but he reached out and grabbed her arm.

"Wait." He couldn't let her leave. The sound of her voice was too soothing.

"Yes?" Joy asked, looking down at him. Once again, he got lost in her eyes. Yeah, there was a *spark* between them and he wondered did she feel it too or was it only him. He silently prayed that it wasn't one-sided.

"Will you be back later? I want to ask you about my condition and how soon it will be before I can get back to work."

"I have to check on my other patients, but I'll be sure to come back before my shift is over, Officer Scott." Joy gently removed his hand and headed for the door.

As Joy was about to leave the room, Marcus came in with a cup of coffee in his left hand looking every bit of the cop in his uniform. He noticed how his partner smiled at Joy before she left his room and closed the door behind her. For some odd reason, the sight of Marcus looking at Joy bothered him, and he didn't know why. It wasn't like she was his. Hell, he didn't even know if she was married or not.

"Man, you must be getting old as me if you can't dodge a bullet," Marcus joked as he sat down in a chair with a paper cup in his hand. The smell of fresh coffee drifted towards Logan making him want a cup for himself.

He would have to ask Joy when she came back if he could have one.

"Stop joking around," Logan complained. "I was supposed to catch Ridge, not end up in the hospital with a shoulder wound like you."

"Don't complain. It was only a flesh wound. You lost so much blood and stayed out so long that they kept you in here an extra day. I think the doctors were checking for a head injury, too, but I told them your skull was too thick for that." Marcus smirked at him before he took a sip of his coffee.

"Great. I hope that means I can get back on the streets faster than you. It shouldn't take my shoulder that long to heal," Logan exclaimed. "I can't wait until I get another chance at Ridge and Luther. I have to get those two off the streets."

"Good luck at that. We can't find them anymore. They both went into deep hiding after shooting you. I believe Ridge is even cockier now than ever. I know he's up to something. If we could only find out what it was."

"Ridge is young, but he's brilliant. With Luther as his cohort, they're a dangerous team. God, Ridge's dad was an ex-sharp shooter in the Army. He was raised around guns. He knows how to use them."

"That's why he went into selling them illegally, but where is he getting his other money from?" Marcus frowned, sitting his cup on the stand near Logan's bed. "I have been talking to people, but no one is giving him up."

"The sooner I get out of this bed and back to work, the faster I can find a way to get Ridge away from the public. He's becoming more a threat each and every day," Logan complained.

Marcus nodded at his comment. "I agree, but where do you want to start?"

"Ridge is loved and feared by so many. It's going to be hard to find someone to turn on him, but I'm going to

28

do it or die trying." That wasn't an only a promise that he was making to Marcus, but a promise he was making to himself, as well.

* * * *

"Nurse Simmons," the voice called out, interrupting her from her work.

Looking up from Officer Scott's chart in her hands, Joy found one of her co-workers standing in front of her. She had gotten so caught up in the file she hadn't even heard Christine approach.

"Yes, Christine. How can I help you?" she asked.

"You have a visitor. I sent her to the waiting room," Christine said and walked away.

"I wonder who in the world is here to see me." Joy placed the file back and headed for the waiting room. She wasn't expecting anyone because no one ever came to see her at work. Opening the door, she stopped in her tracks as the person stood up and came toward her.

"Hey, big sis," Dymond, her baby sister, grinned. "Are you surprised to see me?"

Joy opened and closed her mouth several times trying to get the words out. Her sister was supposed to be in college. She was paying a lot of money to keep her in that private school. What in the world was she doing here? The semester wasn't over for another three weeks. What in the hell happened that Dymond was here instead of there? She worked extra shifts to keep Dymond in that private all girls school.

"What are you doing here? Is something wrong? Have you gotten in trouble again?" The questions just seemed to roll off her tongue. Joy raked her eyes over the black mini skirt and t-shirt her sister was wearing with the words '*I'm sweeter than chocolate*' across the front.

"You know how it is with me and college. I'm not that fond of it. Being around all of those girls is driving me crazy. I never get to see any hot guys," Dymond complained as she hugged her and stepped back. "Can't I transfer here for my last year?"

"We have already had this discussion weeks ago," Joy replied. "My answer hasn't changed since then, Dymond. You aren't transferring here for college. Mom's last wish was for you to attend a good school and *Criswell* is the best."

"I hate it there," Dymond complained. "All the girls hate me because I'm better looking than them. They don't invite me to go out with them or anything. I usually stay in my room on the weekends, and I hate that."

Joy had to admit Dymond's brown café au lait complexion, light gray eyes, and long shady brown hair did give her problems with other girls. But Dymond couldn't help who her parents were. Her mother had loved Bill Richardson, and her sister was the product of their love. However, Dymond did sometimes go overboard with her attitude toward people. She did come across as a bit of a snob.

"If they don't want to be around you, then you don't need them," she told Dymond. "Find some other girls to hang around. There has to be someone at that college you can spend some of your free time with and not get into trouble."

"I can't," Dymond whined. "The popular girls rule the school and if they say 'don't hang around me,' then the other girls won't."

She didn't like the sound of this. Dymond shouldn't be made an outcast. "Do I need to talk to the dean about this? Maybe she can do something."

"It won't do any good," her sister pouted falling down into a chair. "Her niece Stacy is one of the popular girls there, and she'll take her side over mine. Please, let me stay here with you."

"I can't get into this with you right now. I still have another hour on my shift. Can you take a cab back to the house and wait for me there?" Joy was going to get down to the bottom of this situation with her sister, but now wasn't the time. She got a sneaky feeling that Dymond was trying to hide something from her, but what could it be?

Jumping up from her seat, Dymond grinned at her. "I got here with a cab. I'm sure I can get back to our house with one. God, I'm so happy. On the plane ride here, I thought you would shoot me down."

"I'm not agreeing to anything," she quickly cut in so Joy wouldn't get her hopes up.

"I know, but you aren't saying no, either." Dymond spun around and raced out the exit door.

Joy watched her sister go and wondered if Dymond was telling her the entire truth. She loved her baby sister, but she did have a way of twisting a situation so it would fit her and not the other person. Before she left work, she was going to make a call to Dymond's school and find out what was going on.

Chapter Four

I'm used to seeing naked men. It's a part of my job, so why am I bothered by his bare chest? Joy thought as she watched Logan button up his shirt. He was leaving the hospital today, and she couldn't shake the feeling of unhappiness that she felt. She had grown quite fond of the handsome police officer while he was under her care. He always brought a smile to her face anytime she walked into his room.

"Well, you look like you're ready to leave this place," she said, coming further into the room. "All you have to do is sign these release papers, and you're out of here."

Logan finished buttoning his shirt, then glanced at her. "Yeah, I'm happy in some ways and disappointed in another."

"What are you disappointed about?" Joy frowned. "Most people are excited when they get to leave this place."

"Oh, I'm very happy about leaving," Logan grinned. "But I'm sad that I won't get to see your beautiful face anymore."

"Officer Scott, are you flirting with me?" Joy smiled. God, she hoped that he was, because Logan was a very good-looking man.

"Yes, I am. I was hoping you'll go out on a date with me."

He was asking her out on a date. A couple of her male patients had asked her out before, and she turned them down, but she was actually considering saying yes to Logan. "I don't know. I never went out with a patient before. Besides, I thought you were involved with your partner," she replied.

"I know that you mean Peggy and not Marcus," Logan chuckled as he picked up his jacket off the bed. "No, she is only my partner. There isn't anything romantic going on between us. So, does that mean you'll go out on a date with me?"

Holding the release papers against her chest, Joy studied Logan. It had been such a long time since a hot guy had asked her out. Plus, the hours she worked at the hospital didn't give her a lot of time for dating. She would love to say yes, but she had to take care of something important with Dymond.

After talking to the dean at her sister's school, she found out Dymond wasn't telling her the truth about the reason she came home. If Dymond thought she was going to stay here with her and break the rules, her baby sister was in for a rude awakening.

"Can I get a rain check?" Joy inquired, handing Logan the papers along with a pen.

"As long as the rain check isn't too far in the future. I really want to go out on a date with you." Taking the items from her, Logan signed the papers and handed them back.

"Are you always this persistent when it comes to a woman?" Joy chuckled. She really liked how forward Logan was. It was a turn-on in some ways.

"Only when I find the woman very attractive. So is that a yes?" Logan smiled and winked, making her heart skip a beat.

Joy wanted to say no, because she didn't have time to get into anything with Officer Scott. Not with everything that was going on right now in her life. Wait! Why shouldn't she at least go out on a date with him? What was it going to hurt? It might be nice to get away from the house for a couple of hours.

"How about I call you later on in the week, and we can set up a date?" she suggested.

A huge smile spread across Logan's face. "I like the sound of that." Reaching into his jacket pocket, he pulled out a card and handed it to her. "My home phone number is on the back."

Flipping the card over, Joy looked at the number and shook her head. Yes, Officer Scott was something else. It might be a lot of fun to get to know him better. "Do you always have your personal phone number this handy?" She really was beginning to like Logan. He was just *too* cute. He reminded her of that actor who played Doctor Pete Wilder from that show *Private Practice*. She only started watching the program a couple of weeks ago, and he was definitely what kept making her tune in each week.

"I have to admit that I was hoping you would say yes, so I got it ready ahead of time," Logan confessed.

"Okay, Officer Scott. I'll call you when I know my next day off." Joy slid the card into her pants pocket.

"Please, call me Logan. Officer Scott sounds so impersonal. Do you think you can do that for me?"

"I believe I can, Logan," Joy replied and smiled.

"If you can't get me at home, call me at work. One of the guys will find me. I'll make sure that they know you might get in touch with me."

Joy liked how excited Logan was about the prospect of her calling him. She couldn't remember the last time a man had taken such an immediate interest in her like this. Most of the men who worked with her were married or in a serious relationship which made them untouchable in her eyes. She didn't want the same kind of heartbreak her mother got from being in love with a married man.

"Well, I better go. I have a few more patients to check on."

"Those are some lucky patients. I know how much better I felt after finding out you were my nurse," Logan flirted.

"I'm leaving now before it gets too thick in here," Joy grinned and headed for the door. She paused at the entrance, waved goodbye to Logan, and left the room. However, she felt Logan's eyes on her all the way. As she made her way down the hallway back to the nurse's station, she noticed Logan's partner Peggy coming toward Logan's room.

"Good morning, Officer Williams," she said in a friendly voice.

Instead of returning her greeting, Logan's partner brushed right past her without saying a word. She acted like she wasn't even standing in the middle of the hallway. Joy had a nagging suspicion that Peggy wasn't fond of her, and now she knew her opinion was right.

* * * *

"Are you ready to get out of here?" a voice asked him from the doorway.

Moving away from the window, Logan glanced over his shoulder and saw Peggy standing there. He was shocked yesterday when Marcus informed him that Peggy would be the one coming to pick him up from the hospital instead of him.

He knew that Peggy liked being his partner, but she was showing a lot of personal interest in him. He already had a discussion with her a few weeks back how they could never be anything more than partners and friends. Peggy acted like she had understood, and he hoped she hadn't been lying to him.

"Peggy, thanks for coming to pick me up," he retorted. "I really appreciate it. You really didn't have to go out of your way like this."

"Logan, you're my friend and partner," Peggy replied, smiling at him. "I didn't mind doing this at all. Besides, Marcus was busy at work, so he couldn't do it. Do you want to stop by somewhere and get something to eat? I know you must be tired of hospital food."

The only thing he wanted to do was leave the hospital and get home. "No, thanks," he said. "I just want to go home and relax. My arm is still a little sore from the bullet, but my injury wasn't as bad as Marcus'. The doctor told me I should be able to go back to work in two weeks."

"That's wonderful," Peggy smiled. "I have missed seeing you there. The place just isn't the same without you."

"How about we head on out of here and you can fill me in on any news you have about Ridge. I know he hasn't been keeping low while I have been in here. That isn't like him at all." Logan glanced around to room to make sure that he had everything, then headed for the door with Peggy behind him.

"We have been looking for him, but he's nowhere to be found," Peggy said, catching up with him in the hallway. "I think someone is hiding him until the news about the shooting dies down a little more. You know Ridge has friends all over town, because he supplies so many people with illegal goods."

"I know, but we have to find a way to get someone to talk," Logan answered as he looked or a sign of Joy. He wanted to see her again before he left. He hoped that she would call him and set a time and place for their date.

"Hey, are you looking for someone?" Peggy touched him on the arm, drawing his attention back to her.

"No, I was just thinking," he replied looking down at her, but a part of him still wondered where Joy was and what she was doing. He was really drawn to her and hoped she would let them see where this attraction could lead.

Chapter Five

"Dymond, where are you? Why in the hell did you lie to me?" Joy demanded, slamming the door closed behind her. Her eyes landed on her little sister sitting on the couch eating a bag of pretzels.

"Joy, I don't know what you're talking about? I haven't lied to you about anything," Dymond replied, tossing the bag on the table.

"Girl, I have had a long day, and I don't want you lying to my face. I called the school and had a long interesting conversation with the dean. You aren't here for the reasons you told me. You got kicked out of school because you were caught with a boy in your room."

Sighing, Dymond stood up and slid her hands into the back pocket of her mini skirt. "So, what's the big deal? God, those ladies there act like they never had sex before. They need to calm down and let it go. The dean is just mad because it was her son, and she didn't want him sleeping with a black girl."

Joy grabbed the back of the nearest chair and fell down into it before she collapsed on the floor. "WHAT?" she yelled. "You slept with Dean Anderson's son? What in the hell is wrong with you? Why did you sleep with him? Is there something going on that I should know about? Why didn't the college call me about this? I know legally you are an adult, but I still should have been informed about this. I am the one paying the bill there. I shouldn't have been kept in the dark about this."

"Luke is a hottie," Dymond exclaimed, retaking her seat. "You would think so, too, if you saw him. He asked me if I wanted to have a little fun, and I said of course. So, I took him up to my room, and we had some fun. God, he was excellent. He was so good that I think I have sworn off boys my own age. I'm going to sleep with older guys for now on."

I should go over there and shake some sense into that damn girl, Joy thought as she tried to fight off the pounding headache she was starting to get. "What is wrong with you? Why are you doing all of this stuff?"

"Joy, don't be like them and make a big deal out of it. I always thought you were a pretty cool older sister. Don't make me think you aren't now. I'm just being young and having some fun. God, why don't you do it? You're always so busy with work. I know that I have never seen you with a boyfriend. Get out there and live a little. Life is too short to work all the time."

"Dymond, I have responsibilities," Joy sighed trying to calm the anger in her body. She wanted to give Dymond a good education, and this is how her little sister was repaying her? Sometimes that girl acted like she didn't have any sense in her head. How could they be sisters, yet so damn different? "Since Mama died, I have had to take care of you. She wanted you to have a good schooling, and now you have just tossed it away. How could you do that?"

"Mama never loved me as much as she loved you. I was there constantly reminding her of what she lost and could never get back," Dymond tossed back.

"Don't start that again. Mama loved both of us equally. She never played favorites with us. You were the baby, and I was the oldest. That was just how it was." Joy couldn't believe that Dymond was still hooked on that after all of these years.

"Sure, that's what you think. Didn't you hear Mama crying herself to sleep at night because of my dad? She never got over his death. Plus, why did I have to wait until I was eight years old to find out about him?"

"Dymond, Mama wanted you to be a little kid. She didn't want you worrying about stuff like that. Bill loved you from the moment Mama told him about you. I heard him talking to Mama about you when I was a little kid. He was going to marry Mama and become part of our family."

"Yeah, but that didn't happen," Dymond complained. "He died and left us alone. Mama never got over it, and that left you raising me. I loved Mama, but you were the one that looked out for me the most."

Joy knew that Dymond resented the fact that she had a hard childhood because of her looks, but that wasn't any reason to fault their mother or act out the way she had been for the past couple of years. She thought for sure moving her sister out of a public school and placing her in an all girls school would be the best thing. However, it turned out to be the worst idea of her life. Dymond was even wilder than when she left.

"How old is Luke?" she asked trying to get back on topic.

"I don't know," Dymond shrugged. "I guess he's around thirty-two, maybe a little younger. It wasn't like I'm underage or anything. I was attracted to him, and I slept with him. No big deal."

"What is wrong with you? You just turned twenty. There is no way you need to be having sex with him," Joy snapped, jumping up from the chair. "We're going back to that school, and I'm going to have a talk with Dean Anderson. Her son is just as much to blame for this as you are. I pay way too much money for them to kick you out like this."

"No, don't." Dymond rushed over to her and pushed her back down. "I hate that place. I have been there since I was eighteen. I'm not going back there. I only have a couple of classes left to graduate. So, I'm going to finish them up here. I already picked up all the information I need."

She wasn't going to stand for this. The all girls school was the best place for Dymond despite the fact she slept with the dean's son. There had to be some kind of probation that her sister could be placed on for the remaining six months of her semester. Dymond was too wild to be attending college here. She would be dealing with all kinds of problems day in and day out.

Joy knew she wouldn't be able to focus on work with Dymond running around town. Her baby sister loved getting in trouble way too much to stay focused on her classes if she was to remain here.

"I'm not agreeing to this. I'm still your guardian until you turn twenty-one. I will find a way to get you back into *Criswell*."

"God, I hate you. I'll runaway before I go back to that damn place," her sister yelled. "I'm outta here." Snatching her purse off the chair, Dymond ran out of the house before Joy could stop her.

"Damn it," Joy cursed. She knew this isn't how their mother would want them acting toward each other. She didn't know where their sisterly bond went over the years, but she had to find a way to get it back.

"Dymond doesn't understand that I'm just trying to do what's best for her." Dropping her head into her hands, Joy massaged her temple and tried to compose herself before she went looking for her sister.

Chapter Six

"I was surprised when Peggy volunteered to come and pick you up from the hospital when I couldn't," Marcus said as Logan went back to the grill to get the steaks. "Is there something going on between the two of you?"

Using his good hand, Logan flipped over the steaks on the grill and tried to ignore his friend's comment. Marcus had come over for dinner to tell him the latest on Ridge's case. "You know I only see her as my partner. I can sense she wants more, but that isn't going to happen. Besides, I'm interested in someone else."

"Well, did you ask her out?" Marcus questioned, moving on to the bait he just tossed out to him. If nothing else, his best friend loved to give his opinion about peoples' love lives. He was a regular old Dr. Phil, but only in a blue uniform and getting paid a hell of a lot less money.

"Who?" Logan inquired, acting dumb as he placed the T-bone steaks on the dish next to the grill. He loved making Marcus sweat for answers to his questions. His ex-partner was more of a brother to him than a co-worker.

Picking up the plate, he carried it back over to the table and joined Marcus. "I don't know who you're talking about."

"Come on. We haven't been friends for twenty years for nothing," Marcus laughed. "I saw how you looked at that nurse. So, have you asked her out yet? I know how you can get when you want something. Hell, I thought she was pretty sexy myself. She looked like that news anchor Jackie Reid from BET tonight. You probably don't even know who I'm talking about."

"Sorry to disappoint you, but I do know who you're referring to," Logan laughed, taking a seat at the table. "I thought she was a good-looking woman myself, and you're right. Joy does look a lot like her," Logan replied. "However, how do you know that she's the woman I'm interested in?"

He knew that he couldn't keep anything from Marcus, and that is what made them such good partners and even better friends. His buddy had a way of knowing what was going on with him without him saying a word.

"Are you telling me that I'm wrong?"

"Yes, I asked Joy out on a date before I checked out," Logan answered, finally giving in. "However, I haven't heard a word from her."

"Joy." Marcus sounded out the name like he liked it. "She's cute, but I think she might be too much of a handful for you. Don't get me wrong. I like a strong woman, but Joy seems like she won't let you get away with anything."

"It's a good thing you aren't the one who wants to date her," Logan said before he placed a steak on Marcus' plate and his. "I like an independent woman."

"Do you need help cutting that?" Marcus waved his fork in the direction of his plate. "I could cut it into little pieces like my mom used to for me?"

"No, thanks," Logan replied, tossing Marcus a look. "I think I can handle cutting this all by myself. My shoulder isn't as stiff. I'm glad it was only a flesh wound. Now, what do you have to tell me about Ridge?"

"He's up to his old tricks again breaking into buildings and robbing people. Every time we get him into a jail cell, no one wants to testify against him, and he makes bail. I have never known a criminal as lucky as him"

"Damn it. I want to put that punk behind bars. I can't believe no one will point him out of a line up. He has way too much luck on his side," Logan growled. He became a cop to keep guys like Ridge off the streets, and he wasn't doing it. He was pissed as hell. Things had to start working in their favor, or he didn't know what he was going to do.

Marcus nodded. "I'm in totally agreement with you. He has shot both of us, but he always finds a loop-hole out of doing time. I don't know how he has so much damn luck on his side, but it must be someone with some power."

"Ridge is a danger. If we don't get him off the streets, he's going to do a lot of damage," Logan complained, then winced as pain shout through his arm. "I'll be glad when I can get back out there and find him. We have to get someone to stop thinking he's the man because we haven't locked him up yet for shooting us."

"He's already supposed to be locked up for shooting you, but he got away and has been on the run ever since. Plus, when he teams up with that partner of his Luther, I really get scared. Alone, Ridge is a danger, but with Luther, he's more dangerous." Just thinking about how Ridge was able to keep getting out of things was making him lose his appetite.

"It won't do you any good to worry about it, because you can't partner back up with Peggy for another week or two," Marcus pointed out.

"Peggy is a great partner, and I know she's single. Why don't you ask her out? You bring her up a lot."

A sly grin covered Marcus' face. "Oh, are you trying to shove Peggy my way now since a pretty hazel eyed nurse has caught your attention? I never pegged you for the type to date a black woman."

"I think all women are beautiful; however, Joy does have this special quality about her. Hopefully, I'll hear from her pretty soon." If she didn't call him, he would find her phone number and call her. They were going out on a date one way or another.

"Man, you're really taken with her, aren't you? I've seen you interested in women in the past, but *never* this quickly." Marcus took a sip of his beer while waiting for a reply.

"I know, and I wonder why that is," Logan confessed.

Chapter Seven

"Dymond, I've responsibilities. I can't spend half the night looking for you at night clubs," Joy yelled, throwing her purse down on the couch. "You aren't twenty-one yet. How in the hell did you even get in that strip club?"

Rolling her eyes, Dymond crossed her arms under her breasts. "I can't believe you embarrassed me like that in front of everyone. I could have just died."

"You aren't going to put this on me. You're in the wrong here. Damn it, Dymond. I love you, but you can't act like this. If you want to stay here with me, you have to follow the rules. Now, tell me how you got into that twenty-one and over club?"

Her baby sister gave her another hard glare before she slid her hand into her skirt pocket and tossed an item on the living room table. "There. I hope you're happy. My social life is ruined now because of you." Turning around, Dymond stormed from the living room into her bedroom, slamming the door behind her.

Joy wanted to go after her, but she didn't. Dymond hated to follow the rules, but she would have to if she wanted to live under the same roof as her. Bending down, she picked up the item off the table and almost changed her mind about going after her sister.

How in the hell did she get a fake ID? She hadn't been in town long enough for anyone to make it for her, which meant that she got it from *Criswell.*

Maybe I made a mistake by sending Dymond there, she thought. *My sister has been acting out against everything and anything since she started going there.* Could there be something wrong with Dymond and she not even know it? Joy gave the idea a long thought and shook her head.

No, Dymond just loved getting her way, and that was going to stop. She wasn't too proud to take partial blame for it. She and her mother really gave Dymond a lot of attention as a child so she wouldn't miss Bill. Her sister asked numerous questions about her father, and it was a long time before she understood that he wasn't coming back.

"God, please give me the strength to deal with my baby sister," Joy prayed out loud in the empty room. Her mind tried to stay on ways to cope with Dymond and her mood swings, but it kept wandering back to the handsome cop from the hospital.

Logan Scott was a very attractive man. If she had to guess, he was around six feet five inches with a slim build…not quite a swimmer's body, but he was one of the sexiest men she had ever laid eyes on. God, those hazel eyes almost made her melt while he was flirting with her at the hospital. She was secretly dying to run her fingers through all of his thick brown hair, but she quickly shoved down the urges. Yet, she wasn't sure if she would be able to do it a second time. Logan was the complete package, and he was tempting her in ways a man hadn't in a very long time.

Could I really be thinking about calling this guy?

How did she know that he was even serious? He might just be a flirt and pass his business card out to ever pretty women he saw.

No, she wasn't going to think about Logan like that. He came across like a good guy. There was just an honesty about him that made her trust him. Besides, what could one little date hurt? She might get to have a good conversation with an attractive man.

Before she could change her mind, Joy found her purse, dug Logan's card out, and dialed his phone number. It rang a couple of times, and she was about to hang up when a deep voice finally answered.

"Hello?" The warm sound of Logan's voice relaxed the last of the nerves in her body.

"Logan?" she asked.

"Speaking. How may I help you?"

"Hi! This is Joy. Do you remember me?" She hoped that Logan would, because she sure hadn't forgotten about him, despite the problems she had with Dymond earlier.

"Joy, it's so wonderful to hear from you," Logan told her. She could hear the happiness in his rich voice, and it brought a smile to her face. Maybe this was going to turn out better than she first thought.

"I was calling to see if your dinner invitation was still available."

"I'm so glad that you called. I've been thinking about you," he told her. "Yes, the dinner invitation is still open. When would you like for us to go out? Since I'm off until next week, any day this week is good with me."

Joy loved how Logan was asking her to choose the time and day. Her past dates always wanted to determine everything. It was sort of nice the decision was in her hands this time.

"I don't have to work tomorrow. Would you like to meet at *Tyler's* around seven o'clock?" She loved the little Italian restaurant about three blocks from her house. They served the best spaghetti with meatballs. "Do you know where it is?"

"Yes, I love their spaghetti and meatballs," Logan replied. "I eat it at least once a week."

Wonderful, Joy thought. If nothing else, they would have one thing in common. "Okay, I'll see you there tomorrow." She was so excited about her upcoming date. With all the long hours she had been putting in at work to pay for Dymond's tuition, she hadn't put much time aside for herself.

"How about I pick you up? I want to make a good impression on our first date," Logan exclaimed.

Joy made her way over to the couch. Taking a seat, she folded her legs underneath her and relaxed. It had been such a long time since she talked to a man on the phone. "I'd rather take my own transportation since it's our first date."

"Don't you know that I'm trained to protect and serve?" Logan said. "I wouldn't let anything happen to you."

Joy couldn't believe Logan used that line on her. If the sound of his voice wasn't turning her on, she might have laughed at him. "How about this time I'll drive myself and if there's a second date, I'll let you pick me up. Is that a deal?"

There was a long pause on the other end, and Joy thought maybe Logan had hung up. "Joy, I have no doubt there will be a second date between us. I felt the attraction we shared the second I spotted you in my hospital room. Hopefully, this first date will lead to much more wonderful things happening between us. Good night, Joy." The phone call ended with a soft click in her ear.

Pushing the end button on her phone, Joy held it against her chest. Logan was such a surprise. He was very direct and honest. Two qualities she had been looking for in a man but hadn't found until now. She couldn't keep the grin from spreading across her face.

"What put that happy look on your face?"

Glancing up, Joy found Dymond standing at the end of the couch wearing her pajamas. Her sister looked like she was about twelve years old instead of twenty with all the make-up washed off her face and her hair back in a loose ponytail.

"I was planning a date for tomorrow night," she answered.

"You're going on a date?" Dymond asked joining her on the couch. "I can't remember the last time you went out on one. How did you meet him? Is he a hottie? Where are you going? Do I get to meet him?"

Joy waited while Dymond rattled off all of her questions. Ever since she was a little girl, her baby sister loved asking questions. "Okay. Stop with the third degree," she laughed. "I'll give you the information that you want."

"You better not leave anything out," Dymond teased, waving her finger in her face and then placing it in her lap.

Moving around on the cushioned seat, Joy got more comfortable. She didn't have much to tell about Logan, but she would tell Dymond what she knew. "I met Logan at work. He came in with a gunshot wound to his shoulder. Luckily, it was only a flesh wound and nothing serious. I thought he was very nice-looking when I first saw him, but I wasn't going to say anything. However, I guess he felt the same way, too, because he asked me out on a date before he signed his release papers."

"Wow, he must be a hottie for you to break your 'don't date a patient' rule," Dymond chimed in.

The image of Logan's attractive face flashed before her eyes, and Joy had to admit that he was a good-looking man. But that wasn't the sole reason she was going out with him.

"Logan is very handsome, but that isn't the only motivation I said yes to this date. He seems like a very nice man. I want to see if my first impression of him is true."

"How old is he?"

"I think he's forty. Why?" Sometimes Dymond asked her the strangest questions.

"I thought maybe you were trying to get a younger man. I know a lot of my friend's moms are into that now."

Joy had never been attracted to younger men. Mature men always turned her on. It was something about them already being accomplished and knowing their place in the world.

"I didn't think you would be, but I had to ask," Dymond told her. "So where are you going for your date?"

She wondered if Dymond realized that she sounded more like the big sister instead of the younger sister. She thought it was sort of cute. "Logan is going to meet me at *Tyler's*. We both adore Italian food. That's why we thought it would be an excellent place to meet."

Dymond gave her a huge smile, and Joy got an uneasy feeling in the pit of her stomach. Her baby sister hadn't been around her for a while, but she knew that grin. "What are you smiling about? You aren't going to do anything while I'm gone? I won't go on this date if I can't trust you."

Joy didn't miss the look that passed over Dymond's face. She loved her sister, but she was a typical young person always up to something.

"Joy, I know you're worried about me, but I'm not going to sneak into anymore strip clubs. As much as I love watching hot, hard, gorgeous guys dance, I won't go back there. You can trust me."

A huge burden was lifted off Joy's shoulders. Dymond said what she wanted to hear, and she was going to believe her. They had to start to rebuild the trust issue between them, and now was a good as time as any.

"Okay. I trust you not to do anything while I'm on my date tomorrow." Joy hoped she wasn't making a mistake.

Chapter Eight

Sitting in the jam-packed restaurant, Joy glanced at her watch as she waited for Logan to show up. She had gotten here a little early so she could get her nerves under control. She wanted to enjoy her date tonight. She had focused so much time on raising Dymond and her nursing career after their mother died, dating hadn't been a huge part of her life back then. Hopefully, all of that was going to change.

Now that Logan had asked her out, she really wanted to see where it would go. She still couldn't forget how good it felt getting ready for her date. Even Dymond had commented on her excitement.

"Ma'am, would you like to order now?" The unexpected sound of the voice next to her made Joy jump in her seat. God, she really had to stop daydreaming about Logan.

"No, I'm waiting for my date to show up. We'll order after he gets here," she answered, looking at the young man next to her.

The young man smiled showing braces on his teeth. He didn't look much older than Dymond. "Okay, I'll be back over when your date arrives. By the way, you look really hot in that dress," he complimented, taking a quick look at her breasts before walking away.

Joy shook her head at the waiter. She was amazed he just flirted with her. She would have to tell her co-workers about him tomorrow. "I wonder what's taking Logan so long. I hope he knew what restaurant I was talking about and didn't get lost."

"Sorry, I'm late," a voice whispered by her ear. "I got held up at home with a phone call."

Tiny shivers rocketed through her body at the feel of Logan's breath by her ear and the smell of his expensive cologne surrounded her nose. Coming around the table, Logan came into her line of vision. Joy couldn't believe how sexy Logan looked in his black slacks and royal blue shirt. He truly was the word 'hottie' that Dymond used to describe most of the guys she saw.

"You look very nice," she told Logan after he had taken his seat. Nice wasn't the word she really wanted to use, but she couldn't tell him what she was *really* thinking.

"Thank you," he smiled displaying a set of perfect white teeth. "I got a hint of how good you looked when I was coming toward you, so I knew you would look even better face to face."

Joy thought about how good it felt to flirt with a man again. She had really missed this part of her life and was glad to have it back, even if it was only going to be for tonight.

"You're full of compliments. I like that about you, Logan."

"Keep hanging around me, and I hope that you will find something else to like." He winked.

Joy decided to hold back on her comment when she saw the waiter from earlier coming back over to their table. She and Logan both ordered spaghetti with meatballs and extra breadsticks.

"Okay, tell me why someone as gorgeous as you is still single," Logan asked, tossing his menu to the side as the waiter hurried away with their orders. "I know it's an old line, but I would really like to know."

"I had a lot going on in my life, and dating wasn't the first priority," Joy replied honestly.

"So, what's going on in your life that you couldn't date? Nothing can be that important. I love interacting with people. Dating, in my opinion, is one of the best forums to do that particular activity."

"Dymond is that important to me. I'm the only person she has in her life now."

"Is Dymond your daughter?" Logan asked, reaching for the glass of water the waiter left. He took a long sip and patiently waited for her answer.

"No, she's my younger sister. Our mom died when we were young, and I became her legal guardian. I've been taking care of her since my freshman year of college."

Logan studied her like he was trying to read more into what she was telling him. She didn't want to get into too many personal details about her life or business on the first date. For the most part, she was a private person. Some things were private and needed to stay within the family.

"How did you like that? Most teenagers think of attending college as a time for them to party and have fun, but you had a little sister to take care of. How did you manage it all by yourself?"

"Here's your food," the waiter interrupted as he placed their plates down in front of them. She was so caught up in her dinner companion that she didn't even see the young boy coming back with their order.

"Please let me know if you needed anything else." The words were directed to her instead of Logan, but she brushed them off, because Logan's question was hanging in the air between them.

Joy didn't know what to think about Logan's comment. Was he saying that taking care of Dymond took something away from her youth? Taking a bite of her food, she chewed and thought about how she was going to answer him. It was a tough question to only answer with a couple of sentences.

"Are you implying taking responsibility for my sister somehow made me miss out on college parties and my youth was wasted?"

Placing his fork on his plate, Logan wiped his mouth with a napkin and placed it on the table. "No, I think it's wonderful what you did. It takes a very special person to do that and at a young age. You're an amazing sister. I'm really impressed."

"Thank you," Joy replied and smiled. She didn't want to spend the evening talking about herself. She was here to learn more about the intriguing man in front of her.

"So, tell me. Why did you decide to become a police officer?"

"I have always wanted to help people. I knew I wouldn't make it as a doctor, so becoming a cop was the second best thing," Logan answered. "I've been on the force for about fifteen years."

She knew that Logan might not be able to tell her, but she wanted to know. "Did you get shot by someone you were trying to catch? Are they in jail now?"

Logan was pleased that Joy was asking him so much about his job. He couldn't tell her anything about an ongoing case, but it was nice that she was interested in his job and wanted to know more about him. Most of his prior girlfriends loved dating him because of his job, but they didn't ask him much about his cases. Joy was different, and he really liked that quality about her. It was a freshness that he wasn't used to.

"I really can't go into details about a case with you, but I can say that I'm happy to be going back to work. How about we talk about something different?"

"Sure, why not?"

Over the next hour, Joy and Logan discussed a variety of topics ranging between their favorite foods, television shows, movies, and music. Honestly, Joy couldn't stop thinking that this was the best time she had on a date in a very long time. Logan was nice, easy to open up to, and charismatic

"Joy, I really had a fantastic time," Logan said at the exact same time their waiter came to the table with the bill.

"I did, too," she said, reaching for the check.

"No, I'll get this." He took a credit card out of his wallet and handed it to the waiter.

"I could have paid for this," Joy exclaimed, watching as the waiter walked away. She truly loved how cozy this restaurant was. It was the best place in town to come and relax after a hard day of work.

"No, I wanted to pay," Logan insisted. "I had the best night with a gorgeous woman. Paying for the meal was nothing, because I'm hoping it will lead to me spending more time with you."

Getting up from his seat, Logan came around the table and pulled out her chair. "What do you say? Would you like to go out with me again?"

Standing up, Joy didn't have to think twice about Logan's question. She would love to see him again. This date was so perfect. She had to see if they could have a repeat performance. She was about to answer him but stopped when the waiter came back with Logan's credit card. What was up with this guy always disrupting them on the best parts of their date? It was almost like he was doing it on purpose. She waited while Logan placed it back in his wallet and escorted her out of the restaurant.

Walking beside him on the way back to her car, Joy peeked at Logan from the corner of her eye. She loved how good they looked together. It was almost like this night was meant to happen. Everything about tonight was ten times better than she ever thought it would be. This date was almost daring her to see if a second date could turn out better.

"Do I get an answer? When can I see you again? I have to say, the sooner the better."

Leaning against the side of her car, Joy looked up at Logan as the warm night air blew around them. There was just enough of a glow coming from the parking lot lights to highlight their bodies but keep them partially in the dark, too. It was very romantic.

"I would love to go on another date with you," she finally answered. "I have a busy schedule for the next couple of days. I need to get Dymond enrolled for college. She's leaving a private college for one here in town. She wanted to go by herself, but I need to be there to sign some transfers papers and write a check for books. I'll call you in a couple of days. How does that sound?"

"I think I would like it better if I got to set up our second date. I have the perfect spot already in mind," Logan exclaimed, making her wonder what he had up his sleeve. "How about I call you and give you all the details after I get everything finalized?"

"Okay, I can agree to that compromise."

Logan moved back as she opened the car door and got inside. Closing the door, she gave him a quick smile. "I should be getting home. Drive safe, and we'll talk later."

"You, too, gorgeous," Logan said, stepping back as she drove off.

Joy glanced in her rearview mirror and saw Logan was still standing there watching her. It warmed her heart that he cared after only one date.

Girl, you might have a winner with him, she thought.

"I don't want to move too fast with Logan, but I do hope this does turn into something more," she said to herself as she turned the corner and headed in the direction of her house.

Chapter Nine

"Thank you so much for letting me finish my last year of college here," Dymond said, walking beside her toward the car in the campus parking lot. "I'm surprised how easy it was to get my classes transferred here."

Joy loved hearing the excitement in her sister's voice, but she had to understand that there were going to be some things she had to do. She knew Dymond loved being the center of attention, and that wasn't going to, and couldn't, interfere with her new classes.

"I'm glad everything went smoothly at the registrar's office, too, but you know that things aren't going to change."

"I didn't think they were," Dymond sighed. "Your rules are always there. How can I ever forget about them? I'm an adult, but you still treat me like a kid. I hate all of the rules that I have to follow."

Stopping by the car, Joy looked over the roof at her upset sister. "Dymond, if you have a problem, we can get you enrolled in your previous college. I'm sure I can have a talk with Dean Anderson and smooth things over with her. I want you to be happy. However, rules are a part of life. You have to follow them. I don't want your GPA to drop. A good education is very important." It was one the most important traits that their mother taught them from a very young age. She wanted Dymond to be a success like she was. Dymond thought she was hard on her for no reason, but she truthfully only wanted the best for her sister.

"Mama wanted that for both of us, and I'm not going to let you get anything else. Do you hear me? No partying into all hours of the morning. Also, please don't get into any more trouble, especially if the dean has a son here. I don't need any more phone calls at work about you."

Dymond tossed her a hurt look. "You're acting like I don't know how to control myself. Sleeping with Luke back at my old college was something I want to forget. Can't we just let it go?"

"You're right. I have to trust you. You're almost twenty-one. I'm just so used to taking care of you. However, if I give you my trust, you can't abuse it."

"I swear I'm not going to misplace your trust. But you have to realize that I'm growing up. I do want to have some fun. I can't keep my head in an open book constantly like you did when I was younger," Dymond complained. "I'm cute. I'm not going to let it go to waste. I can study and pull in good grades while having fun all at the same time."

Joy shook off the hurt Dymond's comment caused her. She had worked hard to make their mother's final wishes comes true. Their mother didn't want either one of them cleaning anyone's houses for money. Being a housekeeper wasn't in either one of her daughter's futures. Joy remembered her mother telling her that all the time when she was a little girl as she used to watch her get ready for work.

"Listen here. I'm paying for your tuition. If you can't keep up your grades, I'll stop. Then it will be your responsibility. Then you can be the adult you want to so bad. I'm not going to waste money on you trying to impress people. I work hard to give up a good life. Money doesn't grow on trees. Maybe if you made some instead of spending up most of mine, you would understand that."

"I'm sorry, Joy," Dymond apologized softly. "I shouldn't have said those things. I know you work hard to support us. I promise. I'll try my best to stay out of trouble."

"Dymond, that's all I'm asking. I want you to have fun but not at the expense of you getting into trouble at another college. Come on. Get inside the car. I need to get to work." Joy got inside the car and waited for Dymond to join her.

"How about I try to find a job? I know I should be able work one around my classes."

"We can talk about that later at home." Joy started the car and pulled out of the parking lot. She was going to be late getting back to work from lunch.

Chapter Ten

The black BMW drove down the long driveway past the trees and flowers spread out across the grass. The woman ignored all of the other stones places throughout the perfectly cut grass until she came upon the one that meant something to her.

Stopping the car, she grabbed the roses from the passenger seat and got out. It was almost dark, but it was still light enough for her to see where she was going. As she slowly made her way across the lawn towards the headstone, her high heels sunk into the soft ground.

Dropping down to her knees, she brushed off the debris from the headstone revealing a picture underneath. "I can't believe I'm coming here to visit you like this. It seems like you should still here with me and not underneath this cold, hard ground."

With the back of her hand, she brushed a tear away from her cheek and placed the roses on the grave. "Why did you let him break your heart like this? You shouldn't have allowed him to have that kind of power over you. The two of us could have done anything we put our minds to."

The wind picked up, making the woman tuck her long hair behind her ears. "Don't you remember your promise that we'd always be together? What do I have left now? What do I do without you? I'm all alone since you died."

"You shouldn't have left me, but I can't blame you. It's all their faults. I swear that I'll make them pay for what they did to you...to us. They won't be enjoying the lives they have for much longer. I'll make sure the pain they will feel ends up being twenty times worst than mine."

Lying down on the ground, the woman curled up in a ball crying at the injustice done her, vowing to get her revenge any way she could.

Chapter Eleven

"Hey gorgeous," a voice yelled in the distance. "How are you doing? Do you think you can fit me in for lunch?"

Pausing in the parking lot, Joy glanced back over her shoulder and saw Logan strolling toward her. She couldn't stop the leap of pleasure that raced through her body making her heart skip a beat. It had been a couple of days since her date with Logan and she had really missed him. She had spoken to him on the phone a couple of times, but it didn't compare to seeing him in person. Truly, she had missed looking into his gorgeous eyes.

"What are you doing here? I thought you had to be back at work today?" she asked, watching how sexy he looked in a pair of jeans and pull-over shirt.

"My first day back isn't until tomorrow," Logan answered, stopping in front of her. He ran his finger down the side of her face then across her bottom lip. The touch was very light, and it turned her on like hell. What was this man doing to her? All she could think about was having her way with him, and this wasn't like her at all.

"So, I was hoping I could steal you away for a quick bite to eat. I've missed seeing your pretty face," Logan confessed as he removed his finger.

Tilting her head to the side, Joy studied Logan for a few minutes while she debated his suggestion. "Well...I'm a very popular woman. I'm not sure if I can fit you into my busy schedule," she teased back.

"Is there anything I can do to tempt you into giving me a little bit of your time?" Moving closer, Logan slipped his hand along the side of her neck and ran his thumb over her mouth. "The last couple of days have been horrible for me. All I could think about was why didn't I try to kiss you on our first date. At least then I would know what you tasted like, and that could keep me satisfied until the next time I saw you." His gaze traveled over her face searching her eyes.

There was an air of efficiency about him that fascinated her. Her curiosity was aroused way more than it should be, but she couldn't help it. She tried to fight down the dizzy emotions dancing through her body and failed miserably.

"What can you entice me with?" Joy knew she shouldn't have asked the question, but it was way too tempting not to see what Logan had to tell her.

"How about this?" Logan asked tugging her closer to his powerful frame. Inch by inch, his mouth lowered until it captured hers in a slow, soft kiss. It was like he had all the time in the world to learn the shape of her mouth.

Joy quickly tried to swallow her moan, but it was useless as it left her lips and went into Logan's mouth. Standing on tiptoes, she deepened the kiss when Logan let go of her cheek and wrapped his arms around her body.

"Can I take your kiss as a yes?" he breathed against her moist lips.

"Yes," Joy answered. "But only on one condition."

"What is it?" The touch of his hands running up and down her back almost made her forget what she was going to say.

"Let's eat at my house. I have some leftover lasagna from last night, if that is okay with you."

Logan continued to massage her back through her shirt while he thought about her suggestion. The feel of his warm, hard body against hers was a definite turn-on. He could think about her idea for as long as he wanted.

Seconds, hours, or days, and she wouldn't care, as long as they stayed like this.

"I would *love* to have lunch at you house," he grinned, stepping back. "Let me get in my car, and I can follow you back there." Logan gave her another quick kiss and proceeded in the direction of his vehicle.

Not wasting a moment, Joy unlocked her car, got inside, and pulled out of the hospital parking lot. She glanced at her rearview mirror to make sure Logan was behind her before she pulled out.

* * * *

Unlocking the front door, Joy went inside her house and tossed her keys on the end table next to the entranceway. She heard Logan shut the door behind her as she tossed her purse down on the couch.

"Make yourself comfortable while I get everything set up in the kitchen," Joy yelled back at him as she made her ways toward the kitchen.

"Do you need me to help you with anything?" Logan asked her.

"No, you are my guest, and I want you to be comfortable. Why don't you just look around? Honestly, it won't take me that long to get the food on the table."

"All right," he yelled back to her inside the kitchen.

Moving around the room, Logan took in the traces of Joy's personality that he saw when he was around her. He drank in the things he was finding out about the new woman in his life. She was so open and carefree. The mixtures of dark and light furniture with the hints of color added in here and there was a perfect match for how he saw Joy.

She did an amazing job of breaking up her boxy living room by placing the sofa at a widening angle. Instead of having another sofa in the space making it small and cramped, she had added a flower patterned ottoman. It gave the area an extra conversation spot. It looked easy to move and fit the purpose she wanted it for.

Being an avid reader, he loved seeing a huge bookcase against the back wall filled with a variety of books. Maybe after they finished lunch, he would go over there and check out what Joy liked to read in her spare time. Joy's house possessed a warm and inviting ambience that made him want to get invited back here again and again.

"Logan, everything is ready," Joy called out to him from the kitchen table. "I warmed up the garlic bread in the microwave. I hope you don't mind."

"I love any kind of pasta and garlic bread together. They have to be two of my favorite things," he replied, coming into the kitchen and taking a seat at the table in front of the delicious looking food.

"That's so good to hear," Joy exclaimed joining him at the table. "I had a lot leftovers because my sister is always watching her weight. It's not like she isn't already model perfect as it is. Dymond makes sure she just eats enough to stay healthy."

"I know that she can't be any more beautiful than you are."

Taken back by Logan's compliment, Joy didn't know how to respond. Sure, she knew she was an attractive woman, but she never really focused on her looks, because she had too much going on in her life. So, instead of saying anything, she took a bite of her food.

She noticed how Logan watched her for a few seconds before he took a bite of his food. Joy couldn't help but love the moan of pleasure that left his mouth as he swallowed. It was so good to see someone enjoying her cooking skills. It wasn't like Dymond didn't appreciate her meals, however Logan acted like it was the best thing he had ever eaten.

"Did you make this yourself?" He waved his hand over the plate of food in front of him like he couldn't quite believe it. "I know it tastes too good to come out of a box," Logan praised before taking another bite.

Joy nodded. "Yes, I made it. Cooking relaxes me after a long day at the hospital. When I get into the kitchen, I'm in my own little private world. I get it from my mother." She tried not to get choked up after talking about her mother, but her death was still hard to accept, even after all of these years.

"How long has your mother been dead?" Logan asked, shocking her.

"How did you know I was thinking about my mother? I never said I was."

"You got a lost look on your face when you mentioned her. I can tell you loved her a lot." Reaching across the table, Logan placed his hand on top of hers. It was a small gesture of comfort on his part, but he didn't know how much it meant to her.

"She passed away years ago, but Dymond and I couldn't have asked for a better parent. My dad died when I was really young, so I don't remember him at all. My mother told me that he loved me a lot; I wish that I had some kind of memory of him. I have seen pictures, but that isn't the same."

"In addition, Dymond's father died before she was born. However, with the love our mother gave to us, it was like we had both parents. What about you? Are both of your parents still alive?"

"Yes, they are. It will be their fiftieth in a couple of months. I think I'm going to send them on a cruise," Logan answered as he removed his hand off hers. "They been talking about taking a cruise for the last three years. I think it's wonderful that they have stayed together so long with the way the world is today. I don't think I even remember a time that my parents ever yelled at each other. My house was always filled with such love and understanding."

"Have you ever been married before?" Picking her empty plate along with Logan's, Joy got up from the table. It was hard sitting there looking into his eyes when he was staring at her so intently. All it did was make her recollect their kiss from earlier and fantasize about another one.

Sitting the plates to the side on the counter, she started the water for the dishes in the sink. She had to do something to keep her mind off of Logan's sex appeal. Her kitchen was a pretty decent size, however with his large frame in it, it seemed very small and closed in.

I can do this. He won't make me think about stripping him out of his clothes and having my way right here on the kitchen floor.

"No, I have never been married before," a warm breath whispered by her ear making her jump. "Have you ever been married?"

Damn! What was wrong with her? Couldn't she stop daydreaming about this man for one minute out of the day?

She didn't even hear him come up behind her. What was it about this man that made her forget her surroundings? Logan was working his magic on her, and she was quickly falling under his spell.

Turning off the water, Joy slid the plates inside and focused on trying to work on her mind-blowing attraction to Logan. However, it was a battle she was losing more and more because of the time she spent around him. She had been around good-looking men before, but he was totally making her feel like a high school girl with her first crush.

"Do you have an answer for my question?" Logan asked by her ear, running his fingers down her bare arm. "Is there a man in your past that I have to make you forget so you can focus your total attention on me?"

"No, I don't have an ex-husband. I haven't dated anyone in years," Joy replied as she got lost in the sensation of Logan's fingers on her body. Was it hot in here? Or was it her body acting crazy because of the hard, warm body behind hers? Honestly, she couldn't remember the name of the last guy she had dated because it had been so long.

"Joy, look at me." The words came out more of a command rather than a request.

Spinning her around to face him, Logan wrapped his arms around her waist and yanked her body against his hard chest. "Baby, you don't know how much I love hearing that, because I've been dying to kiss you again," he confessed right before his mouth captured hers.

Joy loved how her soft curves molded against the contours of Logan's tall, muscular frame. It was like they had been cut out from a pattern to fit each other perfectly. It was like there wasn't a part of their bodies that wasn't connected. *Did Logan feel the same thing or was he too caught up in the kiss?* She thought about this the second before she wrapped her arms her arms around his neck.

She couldn't stop the little soft purr in the very back of her throat as Logan's hands moved down her back and squeezed her ass. His grip tightened on her as he slipped a hard thigh between her legs and slowly moved his knee back and forth. Instantly her panties got soaked, making her all the more aware of him and her need to have him buried deep inside of her body.

How was it possible that the mere touch of him sent a hot shiver through her body, pushing her to want more and more from him? It was hard for her to calm down, but she did so the kiss could take over her body. Logan moved his mouth expertly over hers. The kiss was slow, drugging, and sizzling hot! It was a deliciousness that she wanted to go on forever.

"What in the hell are you doing?" a voice shrieked, shocking Joy and Logan apart.

Chapter Twelve

Easing away from Logan, Joy hurried over to Dymond as soon as the perplexed look crossed over her face. Without a doubt, her sister was stunned to come home and find her making out in the kitchen with Logan. With the way Dymond had been acting lately, there was no telling what she might say to Logan. Sometimes her sister didn't know how to think first and comment second.

"Dymond, this is Logan," Joy made the introduction as fast as she could. "The guy I went out on a date with. You remember me talking about him. Don't you?" She wondered what Dymond was thinking. Her sister was so good at keeping her feelings hidden until the right time she wanted to say something.

"Yeah, I remember him. What I want to know is why are the two of you making out in the kitchen?" Dymond asked, tossing a hateful look in Logan's direction before looking back at her. "If it was me with a guy, I would get a lecture."

She didn't want this conversation to get any deeper on her sister's part than it already has. She would have a talk with Dymond after Logan was gone.

"Logan, I would like for you to meet my sister Dymond," she retorted. "Dymond, I want you to meet my friend, Logan Scott." The words rushed from her mouth as she tried to ease some to the tension in the room.

"Nice to meet you, Dymond," Logan said.

"Sure," Dymond answered, tossing her backpack down on the kitchen table.

Logan looked back and forth between Dymond and her. Joy could tell that Logan wanted to say something, but he refrained from doing so. Plus, Dymond wasn't trying to conceal the fact she wanted Logan out of their house. She had to do something so this situation wouldn't get out of hand more than it already had.

Just as she was about to find a way to deal with the building tension, Logan placed his hand in the middle of her back, drawing her attention away from her pouting sister.

"Joy, I had a wonderful time, but I need to check in at the station. I got an early release from the doctor. I'm hoping I can get a little work done there today. I'll call you later." Logan gave her a kiss on the mouth, nodded in Dymond's direction, and went out the front door, closing it softly behind him.

"You're dating a cop?" Dymond gasped.

"Logan is my friend. Yes, we are working on a relationship with each other. Do you have a problem with that? I don't see why you really should. I thought you were happy I was trying to get out more."

She truly hoped things would progress further with Logan. He was nice, handsome, and the kind of man she had been looking for. "What's wrong with dating a cop?" she asked, tossing the question out there as it entered her mind.

"Nothing, I guess," Dymond shrugged. "You just don't come across like the type who would want to date a man in blue. I thought you might hook up with one of those hot doctors at your job."

Date a doctor? The thought had never crossed her mind.

No, she wasn't interested in dating anyone at her job. Most of the doctors there were already married with kids. The ones who weren't already had too many women as it was to keep up with. She was sticking with Logan. He was *perfect* for her.

"How did your classes go today?" Joy inquired, changing the subject. She wasn't going to get into an argument about Logan with Dymond. Something has been wrong with her sister the last couple of days, and she was going to find out what it was.

"I guess they were okay. I caught on pretty quickly to most of them." Dymond replied as Joy took a seat at the table. "The professors seem nice enough."

She knew Dymond well enough to know her sister was hiding something from her. It was better to get it out in the open now rather than have it blow up in their faces later.

"Are you going to tell me what is really wrong with you? I know there was something, so don't pretend that there isn't."

Drumming her slim fingers on the table top, Dymond eyed her for a few seconds. "I do want to tell you something, but I don't know how you will take it."

"Lord, please tell me you didn't get kicked out of college on your first day," Joy exclaimed as she tried to stay relaxed. Dymond couldn't have done something this quick to get expelled.

Dymond's familiar eye roll happened before the deep sigh came. "No, I didn't get kicked out. Have some faith in me. I told you I was trying to change," her sister complained.

"I know what you said, but you aren't known to keep your word to me." Joy hated to point out the truth, but she had to make Dymond understand she couldn't play around with her future.

"After I tell you this, I hope I can prove to you that I'm trying to improve myself," Dymond retorted.

Taking a deep breath, Joy tried to prepare herself for anything and not let her sister ride that one nerve she always seemed to find. Dymond was going to tell her before she found out from someone else. Anytime Dymond confessed something to her, it *never* turned out to be a good thing.

"I'm ready. What do you have to tell me?"

"I got a job."

"WHAT?" Joy gasped, stunned. "How in the world did you find a job? Where is it?" She could only imagine what Dymond was up to now. Sure, her sister told her she was going to start paying her own way, but she was shocked that she actually did it.

Chapter Thirteen

Walking into the police station after his lunch date with Joy, Logan paused in the middle of the floor. He looked at everything going on around him. It was like coming home to him. The smell of coffee tickled his nose. The sound of the phone ringing off the hook and his fellow officers talking to each other made him feel at home. He couldn't believe how much he had missed this place. He had to practically beg his captain to at least let him come in for a few hours.

He waved at a couple of men that yelled to him as he made his way over to his desk. Taking a seat, he fanned his hand over the stack of files before picking one up.

It felt wonderful to be back here again. It was something he had missed while his arm was healing. The stiffness had finally worn out of his shoulder, and he was ready to hit the ground running. Yet, he couldn't do anything until the captain thought he was okay to be back out on the streets again with Peggy.

I need to calm down and not jump the gun about this. Everything needs to be done in steps, or I won't be able to make an arrest.

He wasn't able to do anything while he was on sick leave, but he would do as much as he could from his desk until he got the go ahead. Ridge was going to pay for shooting him and Marcus. The citizens of Chicago needed to be able to walk the streets without living in fear of Ridge and his gang. However, the hardest part was going to be drawing him out in the open.

Maybe when they caught Luther, he would turn on Ridge if the District Attorney offered him a deal. Luther already had two strikes against him. A third one would get him sent away. Hopefully, if he got threatened with a long prison sentence, he would give them the information they needed to lock Ridge up for a good part of his life.

"Logan, I heard you wouldn't be back at work until tomorrow."

Looking up from the file, Logan found Peggy standing in front of his desk. He didn't miss the look of pleasure that passed across her face. He knew Peggy was trying so hard to have a relationship with him outside the work place, but that still wasn't going to happen.

The only woman he desired to have something going on with was Joy. The feel of her soft, willing body pressed so closely to his was almost his undoing. Lord, he didn't know how far it would have gone if Dymond hadn't barged in on them. The next time they got together, he had to make sure it was at his place and not hers. He wasn't fond of her sister walking in on them again. Sure, she was an adult, but he still didn't like the idea of her seeing them getting all hot and heavy.

God, he loved kissing her inside her kitchen earlier. It just felt right to be with her like that. He was dying to hear the sound of her sexy voice and find out what happened with Dymond. So after he found out what Peggy wanted with him, he was going to call Joy. It was only right that he check in on her.

Her sister wasn't happy to find him at their house at all. If looks could kill, he would be one dead man. Hopefully, his presence hadn't put more of a strain on their already rocky relationship. Joy handled the situation well. He could tell Dymond was dying to give him a piece of her mind, but Joy stopped it before it happened. He was touched that even though they hadn't been together long, she was already trying to protect him.

"Logan, are you even listening to me, or is your mind a thousand miles away?" Peggy asked, waving her hand in front of his face. "Are you really okay to be back here?" Pulling out a chair, she sat down in front of him.

"Do you think you should take some extra time off? I'm sure that Marcus and I can handle looking for Ridge," Peggy insisted. "He is in so much trouble now, and his options are running out. There aren't too many places left for him to hide or that many people left for him to turn to for help."

Leaning forward, Peggy ran her eyes over his body like she was thinking about how he would look naked. "I just had the most perfect idea. How about I fix you some dinner tonight at my place? Can you even remember the last time you had a home cooked meal? I know how you are. You'd rather sit at home and eat a T.V. dinner than take good care of yourself."

What was he going to do with her? Logan listened as Peggy tried to find a way to get him over to her house. Honestly, he thought by now that she would have figured out that they weren't going to have an intimate relationship. This constant going back and forth with her was getting old. Peggy wasn't a bad-looking woman, but she didn't make him hot and hard in the middle of the night like Joy.

He never woke up covered in sweat after having an erotic dream about Peggy. His mind never thought about her during the middle of the day, despite the fact she was his partner and they spent an enormous amount of time together. The only woman who made him feel those intense emotions was Joy.

"Peggy, thank you for your concern. But truthfully, I'm okay to be here. My shoulder is just a little stiff, and that's all. The captain wouldn't have let me come back if he didn't think I wasn't well enough."

Okay, he dealt with the first part of Peggy's question. Now he had to move on the second part. He was a nice guy and was trying to find the best way to turn her down without hurting her feelings. Peggy was a good woman; however she wasn't the woman for him. "I also want to thank you for the dinner invitation, but unfortunately I'm not able to accept it."

"Why?" she frowned. "Do you already have plans? I can change the day around. I don't mind working with you."

Logan realized that being nice wasn't getting through to Peggy. He needed to be blunt. "I can't accept your dinner invitation, because I'm dating someone."

Peggy stared blankly at him with her mouth open before she closed it and swallowed. Her eyes slightly narrowed as she asked, "Do I know her? Is she someone from the department? How long have you known her?"

Logan wasn't fond of the third degree he was getting. He didn't think or feel like he had to answer Peggy's questions, but maybe if he did this one final thing, it would get her off his back once and for all. "No, she doesn't work for the department. I met her while I was at the hospital."

"It's that nurse, isn't it?" Peggy snapped. "I remember how you looked at her. Wasn't her name Joy?"

Logan was taken back that Peggy recalled that. Even Marcus hadn't remembered Joy's name. Why did Peggy? It was a little strange. "How did you know that?"

"Logan, I'm not a cop for nothing. I pay attention to what is going on around me. I saw how you looked at her in your hospital room. I'm just surprised you would date her," Peggy mumbled underneath her breath.

"Why?" he asked. "What's wrong with Joy? She's a beautiful woman." Logan didn't know if he wanted to honestly hear what Peggy had to say to him. She could be very narrowed minded sometimes.

"Looks-wise, I guess she's okay, but her personality just seemed like she would be a little on the dull side. I thought you would be more attracted to a woman with a little more fervor to her, that's all."

"Looks can be deceiving," Logan countered. "Joy has just the right amount of excitement for me. I enjoy being around her. The more I get to know about her, the more amazing she is becoming to me."

Peggy gave him an incredulous look before she stood up. "If you say so, I guess I have to believe you. Well, good luck with your new relationship. I hope it's everything you want it to be," she tossed at him before walking away and taking a seat at her desk across the room.

"Great," Logan sighed, running his fingers through his hair. "Now I have pissed off my partner. I don't feel like dealing with her nonsense. I tried to tell her on numerous occasions that I wasn't interested."

Looking around the room, he noticed that everyone looked pretty busy, so he decided to take a break and call Joy. He was worried about the way he left things between her and her sister. Dymond didn't seem very pleased that her sister was with him. Logan got up from his chair and made his way outside. Digging into his pocket, he took out his cell phone and made his phone call.

"Hey, how are you doing?" she asked on the second ring. "I wasn't expecting to hear from you today."

He *loved* the sound of her voice. Joy always sounded like she was in a good mood. "I'm doing well, but I was calling to check on you. Are you okay? I was concern about you after Dymond walked in on us."

"Oh, about that," Joy sighed. "She wasn't happy at all. I think she might be a little jealous of you."

Logan hated that Joy's voice was happy one minute and miserable the next. "What happened? What did she say about us?"

"It has been just the two of us for so long. I think she was excited about the idea of me having a date with you, but she wasn't expecting to find you at the house. Dymond is mature at times and immature at other times."

"Do you think we should all have dinner tonight so she can get to know me?"

"Not yet. She's still mad at me," Joy told him. "I need to work things out with her first and then we can set up a day for that. However, I'm glad that you called. I really had a nice time yesterday."

"I did, too. Our kiss was amazing! I went to bed thinking about it and had a very difficult time getting to sleep." He wasn't about to tell her what he finally had to do, but it would have been better if Joy had been there with him. "I was hoping I could see you tonight."

"Dymond has a job now and will be at work. I could come over to your place."

"You don't sound happy about your sister's job? Why?"

"How about we talk about it tonight at dinner?" Joy suggested, softly.

"Baby, you can talk about anything with me," Logan exclaimed. "Let me give you my address." He rattled off the information to Joy. "Is seven o'clock too late for you?"

"No, that's fine with me. I get off work around five o'clock tonight. Do I need to bring anything?" she asked.

"All I need to see is that pretty face of yours, and I'll be a happy man."

"Logan, flattery will get you everywhere," Joy laughed before hanging up.

"I hope so." Logan snapped his phone closed and shoved it back into the pocket of his slacks and went back inside the police station.

Chapter Fourteen

"Is my cooking really that bad? You have barely touched your food at all," Logan asked her. "I can call one of the restaurants and order you something different."

Joy looked up at Logan and shook her head. "I'm sorry. The meal is delicious. I'm just worried about my sister. Dymond always seems to find a way to get into some kind of trouble. She has been doing it since our mother died. I tried to step up and be mother and sister, but I don't think I'm doing a good job."

"Do you want to talk about it? I think I'm a pretty good listener. Dymond didn't come across like a wild twenty year old to me," Logan asked.

Joy wanted to tell Logan about her past, but she just didn't know where to begin. There was so much to tell and she didn't want him to judge her family, but she had to confide in someone about it. "God, I don't know where to start. There is so much to tell."

"I think from the beginning is always the best place," Logan encouraged. Reaching across the table, he placed his hand on tops of hers, giving it a light reassuring squeeze.

"My mom was a good woman. She worked several jobs trying to provide for us. She was absolutely my best friend in the entire world. She became mother and father to me after my dad died when I was around three."

"She was constantly telling me things would get better for the two of us, and one day it did. She had answered an ad in the newspaper for a housekeeper and landed the position the same day. With this new job, she was able to be home with me after school instead of me staying with the neighbor until she got off from work."

"Sounds like your mother loved you a lot," Logan chimed in.

"She did," Joy agreed. "The pay check was really good at her new job, but there were some problems with it."

"What kind of problems?" Joy paused and thought about the best way to approach the subject. Logan may not like what her mother had done, but she was in love and never thought she was doing anything wrong.

"My mother worked for a married couple, Anna and Bill Richardson. I used to hear my mom complain to her friends how mean Mrs. Richardson was to her, always wanting her to work later than she was supposed to. But Mr. Richardson would step in and let her leave at her scheduled time."

"She didn't mean for it to happen. Really, my mother never wanted to be the other woman, but the more time she started spending around Mr. Richardson, the closer their relationship became."

"Are you saying that Dymond's father was your mother's boss?"

"Yes, but he was going to leave his wife and marry my mother. I heard them talking about it one night. He was so pleased about the baby coming. Mr. Richardson was such a nice man."

"Did your mother ever tell you that Mr. Richardson was going to marry her?"

"No, she didn't," Joy answered. "Mr. Richardson told me that he was going to be my new daddy when the baby came."

Logan let go of her hand and leaned back in the seat. "Something happened, didn't it? What aren't you telling me?"

God, this was so hard for her to talk about. She hadn't thought about this in such a long time because it hurt her mother so badly. She could still hear her mother crying. "Mr. Richardson had come by to check on us like he did every night. He was trying to get everything together so he could move all of us in a bigger place."

"You know all about this at eight years old?" Logan asked.

"I used to listen to what my mother talked to him about all the time. She never had a clue that I wasn't asleep. I wanted to know what was going on. Anyway, that night Mr. Richardson came by like he always did, but he and my mother got into a fight. He left. I don't know what it was about. However, later that night, the police came to the door and told my mother that he had died after being shot at the store."

Joy shivered at the memory. She had never remembered seeing her mother that heartbroken before. It still pained her to even think about it. It seemed like the best part of her mother died that night and never came back.

"How did your mother take it?"

"Horrible. All she did for weeks was walk around in a daze. It took her a while to land another job, but she did. After Dymond was born, she got it together a little better and found a better job."

"Dymond got so spoiled the instant she was born. I loved being a big sister, and my mother adored Dymond because she was made from the love she shared with Mr. Richardson. Maybe that's the reason my sister is the way she is. We gave her too much attention at a young age," Joy confessed.

"When did you tell Dymond about her father?"

"I guess Dymond was around eight years old. There was a father/daughter dance at her school, and she wanted to know why her daddy couldn't take her. My mother volunteered to go, but Dymond said no."

"My mother's health started going bad a few years later when I got into college, and she died leaving me with custody of Dymond. A part of me always wondered if it was something more. I know she never truly got over Bill dying the way he did. If they hadn't gotten into a fight, he would still have been at the house with her."

"I tried to keep my sister in school here, but she just didn't want to listen. So, I sent her off to boarding school thinking it would be the best thing for her, but she gets into trouble there too. I am about at the end of my rope with that girl," Joy sighed. "I know Dymond knows what she's doing. She likes pushing my buttons, and it isn't going to work anymore."

"Do you think me coming into the picture will make things worse between the two of you?" Logan's voice held a hint of concern in it, which concerned her.

"No, I think Dymond will get used to you, and everything will be fine," Joy commented with more bravado than she actually felt. Her baby sister could be hell on wheels when she wanted to.

Getting up from the table, Logan tugged her from her seat and pulled her into his arms. "I want you to know that I love being around you. You're gorgeous, sweet, and funny. I'm willing to let Dymond get used to the idea of us dating, but I won't let her chase me away from you."

"I don't think Dymond will get that bad," Joy interjected. "I'll have another talk with her."

"I hope you're right, but I see it getting worse before it gets better," Logan told her, voicing her silent fears.

Chapter Fifteen

Logan had gotten up early to come to work hoping that something new would be in about Ridge or, at least, Luther. He hated when he felt like he had wasted his entire morning, but it was turning out that way in his mind. All he needed was a break and he knew it would only be a matter of time until everything else fell right into place for him.

"I can't believe no one has seen him," Logan complained, tossing the thick manila folder down on his desk. "I'm tired of people lying to our faces. I know these people know where in the hell he is."

"Man, you know Ridge has a lot of thugs that will protect him from the cops. Some of those idiots are even willing to go to jail for him. I just don't understand it. Are their home lives so bad that jail seems like a better option? It amazes me how kids band together nowadays out of loyalty. I know I did it some when I was younger, but I would have never gone to jail for any of my friends. Yeah, we were close, but not that close," Marcus complained as he looked up from the rap sheet he was reading.

"You know how it is out there with those street kids. It only takes one to step up to the leadership role and the weaker ones will fall in line. Look at Luther. He'll do anything Ridge tells him. Neither one is thirty years old yet, and their rap sheets are as long as my damn arm."

"I know, but none of that is helping us find them. I'm pissed as hell that Ridge is still out there, probably mocking us. I don't understand how that little jerk gets so many breaks from the law. Every time his court cases come up, he only gets a small sentence. I will find someone soon that isn't willing to go down for him," Logan complained. "Anyway, I can't afford to be taking my job home with me. I'm having enough problems in my personal life as it is without adding Ridge to them."

"Is Joy's sister still having a problem with you?"

Not being able to take it anymore, he finally confided in Marcus about Dymond's intense dislike for him. He didn't have a clue where it stemmed from. He never said a mean word to her. However, Dymond acted like he was worse than getting a tooth pulled.

"It's not going well. I was over there yesterday, and Dymond left the second I came through the door. I know it's hurting Joy, but she's trying to pretend that it isn't. I think she might truly hate me, and if I don't find out why, Joy might dump me because of it."

Logan hated that Dymond wasn't fond of him. He had been dating Joy for only a couple of weeks, but she was becoming very important to him rather quickly. He always found a way to be in contact with her, no matter what time of day it was. Just the sound of her voice could brighten his day. He had a date tonight with Joy. God, he prayed that Dymond was in a good mood, or Joy's mind would end up being on her sister instead of him.

* * * *

"Can I talk to you?" Joy stood in the doorway of her sister's room and watched as Dymond got ready for work. "We haven't said much to each other all week."

"I have been working, and you don't spend much of your free time with me anymore. You're always with Logan," Dymond tossed as she pulled her hair back into a tight ponytail.

Wonderful… This is the opening she had been looking for with Dymond. Maybe now she would find out why her sister detested Logan so much. It just didn't make any sense how Dymond practically hated the sight of him.

"What is your problem with Logan? He's a nice guy and I like him. I thought you wanted me to get out and date more. Isn't that what you told me?" Joy clearly remembered her sister almost pushing her out the door for her first date with Logan several weeks ago. "Do you have a problem with him being a cop?"

"I could care less what he does for a living," Dymond exclaimed, rolling her eyes.

"Does him being white bother you then?"

"God, stop acting like I'm a child. I have dated and slept with plenty of guys, and fifty percent of them were white."

"Fine. Then tell me why every time Logan comes over here, you find a way to leave. It's beyond childish and rude on your part. I thought better of you. He wants to get to know you. I'm in a relationship with him." Joy was about at her wit's end with Dymond's snappy attitude. Her sister was acting like she was eight years old instead of twenty.

"Joy, I don't have time to get into this," Dymond complained, totally ignoring her question. "I'm going to be late for work. You were the one who told me I needed to get a job. I did. Now, I need to go before I get fired."

Brushing past her, Dymond tried to go out her bedroom door, but Joy grabbed her sister by the arm. "What's wrong with you? We used to be so close. You can tell me what is bothering you. I love you, and it's tearing me up to see you like this. I can cancel my date with Logan. You can call in sick, and we can just stay home and talk to each other. I'm here for you. You know that, don't you?"

Gray eyes searched her face like Dymond was trying to read her thoughts. Shaking her head, her sister shook off her touch. "I can't get into it with you. You just wouldn't understand. Have a nice time on your date with Logan," she sighed. "I'll try to get better when it comes to him, but I can't make you any promises." Without looking back, Dymond headed out of the room. A few seconds later, the sound of the front door closing reached her ears.

Joy knew there was something going on with her sister, but she just couldn't put her finger on it. The one thing she had loved the most about Dymond was how she openly expressed her opinions. It wasn't like her to keep things bottled up like this. Something wasn't right about Dymond's attitude toward Logan, and she was going to find out what it was, no matter how long it took.

Chapter Sixteen

"Do you know that I thought you were the most beautiful sight I had ever seen when I opened my eyes at the hospital?" Wrapping his arms around Joy's waist, Logan tugged her back against his chest.

After a lot of coaxing on his part, Joy finally decided to leave her house and come over to his. She was trying not to bring up her sister, but he could feel something might have happened between the two of them today. So, until she was ready to talk, he was going to shower compliment after compliment upon her.

"Oh, I bet you tell that to all of your nurses," Joy joked back, resting her head against his chest.

"No, you are the only one to receive that honor. I know that we have been dating for only a few weeks, but I feel like this can grow into something deeper." Logan was beyond ready to take it to the next step, but he wasn't going to push Joy into anything she wasn't ready for.

"You sure do know how to make a woman feel good." Turning in his arms, Joy linked her arms around his neck. "I think I might keep you for a while."

You better believe you are, Logan thought to himself.

"I like the sound of that. Does that mean I might get to see what you wear under that sexy nurse's uniform? I have been thinking about it for a while. However, I don't think my dreams are doing you justice."

"What makes you think I wear anything sexy under my uniform? It could just be a plain old white bra and matching panties?" Joy challenged.

Joy had to be kidding him. *Wasn't she?* With her smooth mocha skin, hips that tapered into long straight legs and her full breasts, Joy was a breathtaking sight in his eyes. Even her short pixie haircut had his heart rate speeding up every time she was around him. Hell, he wouldn't doubt that every doctor at the hospital was probably in love with her, along with a constant state of arousal. All he cared about doing was tossing her down on the nearest bed and having his way with her delectable body. Yet, none of them better ever touch her, or he would arrest them on the spot and toss their asses in jail.

"Are you planning to let me find out in the near future?" he asked, cupping Joy's firm ass in his arms. Logan yanked her against his body, showing her how much he was dying to get to know her on more a personal level.

"Logan, we haven't been together that long. I just can't give it to you so quickly. I want to learn more about you. I told you about my family, along with our past. When am I going to get to know more about you? I think it's only fair."

Lowering his head, Logan brushed his lips over the sensitive spot below Joy's left ear. He learned by accident that this spot made her melt in his arms. "I had a dull life with three other siblings and two parents," he breathed against her skin.

"Can we get to the good stuff now?" He moved his hand recklessly up and down her back. It was getting harder and harder for him not to find a way to seduce Joy into his bed. He had never felt such a strong pull toward a woman before.

"Logan you need to stop," Joy moaned, squirming around in his arms. "Honestly, tell me more about your life. I know you probably did some wild stuff when you were younger."

Moving his fingers back up her body, Logan's warm calloused hands cupped her chin in his palms. "I'm attracted to you. I haven't made a secret of that. I want us to get closer." He wasn't afraid to admit he wanted to move to the next step in their relationship.

Joy's eyes fluttered for a few seconds like she was weakening with his words. "I'm attracted to you, too. I would love for us to make love, but I just want us to learn about each other some more. Come on, tell me about your family."

Logan saw that tonight wasn't going in the direction he had hoped it would. Besides, Joy was right. He needed to tell her more about his life. It was only fair, since she opened up so much about her childhood.

"Come with me." Going over to the couch, he got into a comfortable position and pulled Joy down between his legs, resting her back against his chest. It just felt so right having her here in his arms. Sure, he was ready to make love, but he could wait.

"Okay, what do you want to know about me?" he inquired.

"Will you really tell me all your deep dark secrets?" Joy asked, playing with the hair on his arms. "I'm kind of greedy. I might take all you have to offer."

"It depends on what you want to know," Logan answered honestly. Joy possessed an air of calm and self-confidence, which he liked and admired.

"Like I said, I want to know everything about you. Tell me how you were as a child. Do you have any favorite foods that you crave in the middle of the night? Do you sleep naked? Who was your first kiss? Better yet, who was the first woman you slept with? Anything you want to tell me, I want to hear."

He loved that Joy was interested in the deepest part of him. It meant that things were going better between them than he first thought. They might be headed for a deep commitment, and he was thoroughly pleased with this possibility. His body seemed to instantly relax after the thought settled into his mind. Now he could tell Joy all...well, maybe not all the things she had asked about.

"I'm the oldest of three children. We were raised in New York City until I was about eight years old and then we moved here to Chicago. I did okay in school. I wasn't the worst student, but I wasn't the best either. I played basketball from my freshman year in high school until my senior. I went to college on a basketball scholarship."

"My brother has worked as an art teacher for the past twelve years at the local college in town. My younger sister works at a law office as a paralegal. Both of them are married with three kids each. After spending a day with them, I almost don't want kids, but I always change my mind."

"I hate to admit it, but David and I tormented Ariel horribly when we were kids. I don't know how many times we hid her dolls from her," he laughed at the memory. It had been such a long time since he thought about that.

"Shame on you for being mean to your sister," Joy cut in, hitting him on the arm. "I bet you left her in tears."

"Are you saying you never teased Dymond when you were younger?" he asked by Joy's ear as he ran the tips of his fingers under her breasts.

"Okay, I did," she giggled pulling at his hand.

He felt a warm glow flow through him at the sound of Joy's laughter. He was so happy she was so relaxed with him tonight and not worried about Dymond. Yes, Dymond was her baby sister, but her every emotion shouldn't be tied up with her. She needed to let Dymond make some mistakes and learn from them, or she wouldn't be able to grow into a responsible adult. It was hard for him to do the same things with his siblings, but he eventually did.

"What else do you want to confess?"

"Why do you think I have any more confessions?" he inquired, thinking about everything he was dying to share with Joy.

"You're a very attractive man. I love dark hair and brown eyes. I know I'm not in the minority when it comes to your looks. I have no doubt you have something juicy to tell me."

"I'm not sure about something juicy to tell you, but I definitely have something very hard to give you." Moving his hips, Logan brushed his erection against her. "How about it? Do you want a taste of what I'm offering?"

Slipping his hand underneath her shirt, he played with the skin not covered by her bra. If everything worked out the way he planned, he had every intention of making Joy fall under his spell.

"You're such a bad boy," Joy moaned writhing in his arms.

"Let me show you how bad I can be," he encouraged by her ear. "Come on, let's make out for a while. Don't you want to?" Moving his hand up a few inches, he covered Joy's full breast and played with her nipple.

"You have to stop," she said again. However, the words sounded weak to his ears. Joy was dying for this just as much as he was.

Chapter Seventeen

I can resist him. I need to do this. Things are going too fast between us. We need to slow down. I'm not used to this burning passion, Joy thought as Logan worked on the front latch of her bra.

"Baby, you are so soft. I could touch you all day and never find a reason to stop," Logan whispered next to her ear. His words were making her think things that she shouldn't. She was more of a woman who thought things out than jumped into a situation with both feet.

"I would love for you to touch me all night long, too," Joy confessed, letting her body take over her mind for a moment. "But I can't do it. I need to leave."

"Joy, stay a little longer," Logan's deep voice coaxed. "I swear it will be worth your while."

She didn't have a chance to answer before Logan flipped her over so her back was on the couch and he was above her. Seconds later, her top and bra were on the floor, and his wet hot mouth was sucking on her hard nipple.

A flood of moisture saturated her underwear. "Oh, my God," she screamed running her fingers through the thick cool strands of Logan's dark brown hair. She hadn't been this close to a man in such a long time. Damn, it felt good knowing her body was still alive and ready to get some action.

Tiny electrical shocks zipped over her as Logan pushed up her short skirt and brushed his erection against her damp underwear. She spread her legs wider, giving him better access to her lower body.

"That's feels so good," she whimpered, pulling at Logan's shirt.

Letting go of her nipple, Logan stared at her with desire-filled eyes, making her moan under her breath. Shit, she wanted his man. It was getting harder to resist him, but they have only known each other for such a short period of time. Was it right for her to want to spend the rest of the night and all day tomorrow in bed with him?

"I can make it feel even better," Logan replied. Raising his body up, he tugged his shirt over his head and tossed it on the floor before covering her body with his again.

"I'll believe it when I see it." Joy ran her hands over the top of Logan's shoulder, enjoying how his sweaty skin was making her even hotter.

"How about I make you feel it instead?" Grabbing her hands in one of his, Logan pulled them above her head and then dropped his head running his tongue across her collarbone and thrust his cock against her moist heat.

Yes! Oh, Yes! Joy's mind yelled as she moved her hips against Logan's denim-clad erection. Why was he teasing her like this? He knew she was dying to have him buried deep inside of her.

"Please," she begged pulling at her arms.

"Please, what?" he asked as his tongue slowly licked its way down to her nipple. "Do you want me to do something, sweetheart?"

"YES!" Closing her eyes, she tried to get lost in the sensation of Logan's body loving her. It wasn't exactly what she was craving, but it would have to do for now.

"Tell me, Joy. Do you want me to strip you out of this wet underwear and slide my thick cock inside of you? Is that what you want, baby?"

He was taunting her on purpose. She should hate him for it, but it was making her even hornier! Damn him to hell. Logan was getting a thrill out of using her body against her. She would get him back later, but now wasn't the time. She had to get him inside of her now.

"You know that is what I want. Why aren't you doing it?" Joy opened her eyes and glared at Logan. He was beginning to make her want to take matters into her own hands.

Removing one of his hands from her wrists, Logan skimmed his fingertips across her body until they stopped at the top of her skirt. "I thought you told me a few minutes ago that you wanted to take things slow. I wouldn't dream of influencing you to do something you didn't want to. Maybe we should stop. I can tell you more about my childhood."

No, he didn't just tell her that he wanted to stop! *What in the hell was wrong with him?* She wasn't going to let him do this to her. She was on fire for him, and he would give her what her body was dying for.

"Yeah, I think I need to stop," Logan exclaimed as he eased his body away from hers, taking his wonderful body heat. "I'm going to listen to you instead of my body. It's only fair that I do what you want."

"Don't you dare move," Joy retorted, wrapping her legs around Logan's waist pulling him back onto her. "I want this. You don't know how much I want this."

"What do you want?" he asked as his thumb played with her bottom lip.

Heat started in her stomach and burned its way through her entire body. She was usually so strong, but when it came to Logan's touch, she turned into a puddle of mush.

"You know what I want. Don't make me say it," she moaned, softly.

"I'm not a mind reader, baby. You *need* to tell me so I can get it right."

He's playing with me. I can't believe it. I'm craving to have him buried deep inside of me, and Logan is asking me what I need.

"Does the cat have your tongue?" he teased. "Do I need to give you a hint?" Unwrapping her legs from around his waist, Logan spread them as far as they would reach before rubbing his denim-clad cock against her soaking underwear.

"Oh," she purred lifting her hips. "That feels *so* good."

"Good," Logan frowned, staring down into her eyes. "I've got to up my game." Dropping his head, he nibbled at her breast before pulling her hard nipple into his warm mouth.

The sensation of Logan's lips on her breast was too much for her to handle. As she was about to reach her orgasm, a loud banging on the front door shocked them apart. Logan glanced down at her then his eyes swung over toward his front door as the sound got louder.

"Who in the hell is that?" he growled as the rapping continued.

Shit! Why did this have to happen now? It was getting so good. She couldn't remember the last time she had an orgasm, and it didn't seem like tonight was going to change that, either.

"I don't know, but maybe you should answer it," she retorted. The romantic mood of the night was over. She couldn't get back into this with Logan. Now with someone right outside the door, it was just too weird for her. Anyway, it didn't seem like their visitor had any plans of going away anytime soon.

"Ignore it," Logan whispered trying to kiss her.

"No, we can't," Joy sighed, shoving at his shoulder. The mood was already ruined. There was no reason trying to get it back now. The person on the outside was going to break the door down to get inside to Logan.

Dropping his head into the crook of her shoulder, Logan let out a deep breath as he tried to get his body back under control. He didn't seem anymore happier about their surprise guest than she did. Whoever it was truly had a bad sense of timing.

"Logan, are you in there?" a female voice yelled through the door.

Joy's body froze at the sound of the unwanted voice. What in the hell was going on? Was Logan making out with her while he had another woman on the side? No, she wasn't going to jump to conclusions. She would ask him directly instead, and he was going to give her an answer.

"Who is that?"

Logan gave her a quick kiss on the mouth before he untangled his body from hers. Standing up, he picked up her clothes and gave them to her. "My partner Peggy," he replied, snatching up his shirt and pulling it over his head.

"Does she always come by here so late?" she asked as she got redressed. She didn't want to be jealous, but a part of her was. Logan's partner was an important part of his life. He probably spent more time around Peggy than he did with her.

"She's probably here about the case we are working on," Logan informed her as he headed towards the front door. "Are you ready to meet her?"

"I guess so," Joy replied wondering what Peggy's reaction was going to be. The woman she remembered from the hospital wasn't nice to her at all. She wondered if now was going to be any different.

"It will be fine," Logan winked at her and opened the door. He hoped that what he just told Joy was true, because he wasn't ready for anything else to happen inside his living room.

****

"Peggy, I'm surprised you are here this late," Logan stated.

"I almost left," Peggy said brushing past him as she came into the house. "What took you so long to answer the door? I have some new information about Ridge. He has been spotted. Shut the door, so I can..."

Peggy stopped talking when she spotted Joy standing next to the couch. He could almost hear Peggy's body tense up as she tried to control her reaction at finding Joy at his house. She wasn't pleased at all. He didn't have to wonder if she was jealous. He could see from her body language that she was. "I didn't know someone was here with you."

Logan watched as Peggy raked her eyes over Joy giving her the once over. Without a doubt, he could tell this wasn't going to go well between his new girlfriend and Peggy. Peggy was very territorial when it came to him. She truly believed that she was the only woman that should be in his life. He needed to have another talk with her about not crossing the line when it came to his personal life.

"I guess now is the best time to introduce the two of you," Logan sighed as he closed the door and made his way over to Joy. Planting a kiss against the side of her head, he wrapped his arm around her waist.

"Joy Simmons, I would like for you to meet my partner, Peggy Williams. Peggy, this is my girlfriend, Joy Simmons." He waited while the women seized each other up. He was just dying to see which one would make the first move.

"Nice to meet you," Joy smiled as she extended her hand for Peggy to shake.

That's my girl, Logan thought.

Secretly, he was very proud that Joy made the first move toward being friendly instead of Peggy. It proved he picked the right woman to be in his life. However, as the minutes ticked by, he grew more pissed as he watched Peggy's eyes narrow at Joy's hand before they swung back up and looked at him. He prayed that Peggy wasn't going to insult Joy, because if she did, he would make her apologize instantly. She had no claim on him to be acting like this.

"I didn't know that you had moved to girlfriend status," Peggy said giving Joy's hand a quick shake before letting it go. "You're a very lucky woman. Logan is an outstanding guy. I don't think the world makes men like him anymore. At least, I'm not lucky enough to have found one. You better hold on to him with both hands before another woman steals him away."

Logan heard the jealousy mingled with hate in Peggy's tone. He wondered if Joy picked up on it, too. Hell, Peggy just practically told Joy that she wanted him for herself.

"I can't disagree with you. Logan is a keeper, and I'm planning to hold on to him for a very long time. I would be out of my mind to let him go and have a less deserving woman snatch him up. Don't you agree?"

If he ever thought Joy was oblivious about Peggy's feeling toward him, her comments just proved him wrong. She was willing to fight for him, and it was really turning him on. Logan dragged his attention away from his inner thoughts back to the conversation going on around him.

"It's good to know that you understand what you have," Peggy flung back.

"Oh, I understand what I have, and I'm not about to lose it, either," Joy tossed back with equal passion.

Turning her attention away from Peggy, Joy looked up at him. He could see the anger simmering behind her eyes. Oh, she was pissed! What in the world was she going to say to him? He just took a deep breath and waited.

"I think I should go so your partner can talk to you."
Moving away from him, Joy grabbed her things out of the
chair by the couch and went for the door.

"Wait, let me walk you out." Logan hurried past
Peggy and escorted Joy outside. He wasn't about to let her
leave mad at him. He had nothing to do with Peggy
showing up unannounced and ruining their romantic night.
Shit, if he had gotten a few more minutes, he would have
been doing something totally different with Joy now
instead of walking her out to her car.

He wondered what was going on in Joy's head. He
thought that Peggy's body language was speaking volumes
inside, but Joy's body language was twenty times worse.
She was outraged by the way Peggy had treated her, and
so was he. He would definitely have a talk with her, but
first he had to apologize to Joy.

"Baby, I'm so sorry about what happened back there.
Peggy had no right to act like that. She has no reason to act
like that about me."

"Have you slept with her? Tell me the truth. No
woman acts that resentful unless you have been with her."
The question came out of left field, shocking the hell out
of him. "Is that why she is so possessive?"

Leaning back against the car door, Joy folded her
arms over her chest and gave him a pointed look he didn't
like. *What was wrong with her*? He had never looked at
Peggy as more than a coworker and capable partner in all
of the years she had been at the station. He wasn't about to
mix business with pleasure unless Joy changed careers in
the near future.

"Sweetheart, you have nothing to worry about. I only
see Peggy as my partner. There have never been anything
romantic between the two of us, and that isn't going to
change." Undoing Joy's arms, Logan wrapped them
around his neck and placed his hands on her waist.

"I love that you were jealous. It does a lot for my ego," he chuckled.

"I wouldn't be so smug," Joy teased. "Or I'll send you back in there to that Linda Hamilton wannabe."

"Linda Hamilton, you mean that chick from those Terminator movies? You think Peggy looks like her?"

"You don't?" Joy inquired, arching an eyebrow. "They could pass for twins. Peggy would probably send Arnold after me if she could. I know she wants you."

"It doesn't matter what Peggy wants," Logan exclaimed softly. "I only have eyes for one woman. Do you know who she is?"

"I'm going to take a wild guess and say me."

"Give this lady her present," Logan whispered right before he kissed Joy. The kiss only lasted a few seconds, because he knew Peggy was waiting for him with information about Ridge.

"I need to go," he breathed against Joy's moist, swollen lips.

"Go on. I'm going to make a quick stop at Dymond's job and head on home. It's really late and I need to get up early for work."

"Will I see you tomorrow?"

"I doubt it," Joy sighed, shaking her head. "I have to work double shifts at the hospital. How about we get together on Wednesday? I'm off for the entire day."

Logan groaned under his breath. "I can't. I'm working all day. God, I can't imagine being without you for two whole days. What are we going to do?"

"I don't know, but I'm sure you can find a way to make it up to me once we get to see each other again," Joy exclaimed, then placed a quick kiss on his mouth. "Now, you better get back in there before Peggy comes out here to get you."

Joy gasped as Logan yanked her close to his body and slid his hand behind her neck. "Woman, Peggy is the last person on my mind right now. I can't let you leave without giving you a proper goodbye kiss," he growled before his lips swooped down and captured hers.

The warmth of his mouth was intoxicating. A spurt of hungry, wanting desire spiraled through her body. She could feel the heat of his body as Logan pressed her against his hard length. Joy knew that she wanted to stay out here with Logan, but they couldn't.

Slowly, Joy eased her mouth away from his and pushed Logan back. "We have to stop before that kiss gets out of hand."

"What's wrong with things getting out of hand? I love a little excitement in my life, don't you?" Logan asked as he reached for her again.

"I do, too, baby. However we both have things that we need to take care of tonight."

Mumbling under his breath, Logan looked at her like he wanted to disagree with her. "I hate to admit it, but you're right. I really do need to discuss this case with Peggy."

"See, I'm glad I'm the level-headed one in this relationship." Digging her car keys out of her purse, Joy unlocked the door and got in, closing it behind her.

"Will you at least call me in the next two days?" Logan inquired. "I won't be working so hard that I can't talk to you on the phone. At least, I will have the sound of your sexy voice to tide me over until I see you."

"Don't pull that little boy act on me," she laughed. "You know that I'll call you before the night is over. Just give me time to take care of some personal stuff." God, she was already counting the seconds until she heard Logan's voice on the phone.

"I'll be waiting for your call, beautiful." Leaning through the open car window, Logan gave her a quick kiss and stepped back.

"You'll get it," Joy promised Logan before she started the car and drove off.

****

Logan stood outside and let the cold air cool off his heated body. He didn't want Peggy to think she caused his ragging erection. For some reason, she couldn't seem to understand that he wasn't interested in her in a romantic way and that wasn't *ever* going to change with him.

Turning on his heel, he headed back toward his house and went inside. The door hadn't closed behind him before Peggy's tirade started. "I didn't come all the way over here to tell you about Ridge to be kept waiting. It doesn't take ten minutes to tell someone goodbye," she complained.

"You were timing me?" Logan frowned. He wasn't pleased that Peggy was paying attention how long he was outside with Joy. It really wasn't any of her business. "I can't believe you were doing that." Moving away from the door, he took a seat in a chair across from the couch.

"I wasn't planning on it, but you were taking so damn long with Joy." Peggy left her spot by the window and sat down on the couch. "Like I said when I first got here, I have new information about the case."

"What is it?" He hoped that it was something that would finally get Ridge some prison time.

A gleam came into Peggy's eyes as she leaned forward and stared into his eyes. "Ridge was spotted tonight coming out of a convenience store. Someone called the tip hotline."

"Was it a positive ID?"

"The caller wasn't a hundred percent. So, I went to the convenience store and showed the worker there a picture of Ridge, but he couldn't tell me either way."

Fuck! He was hoping for something more than that. Ridge has been a thorn in his side for far too long. It was time that punk was off the street and away from tax-paying citizens. "Do you think it could have been him?"

Peggy nodded her head in agreement. "Yes, it would be the kind of place he would stake out before he robbed it," she stated.

Logan wasn't as thrilled as Peggy was about the tip. Ridge was smart. He wasn't letting anyone notice him unless he wanted them to. So, what was Ridge up to and why wasn't Luther with him? Those two were like two peas in a pod. They never went anywhere without each other.

Ridge was planning something, but what was it?

Chapter Eighteen

The next morning, Joy relaxed at the kitchen table drinking a glass of orange juice when Dymond waltzed in. She approved of the jeans and sweater her sister was wearing. Over the past couple of weeks, Dymond had started dressing better, which meant showing less skin. Maybe her little sister was finally deciding to grow up since this was her last year of college.

"Do you want to stay home with me tonight and watch the presidential debate? This is the last one before the election."

"I wish I could, but I have already agreed to work an extra shift. I need the extra money for my books since I added a journalism class. I didn't realize three extra books would cost that much," Dymond complained, grabbing a banana off the table. "Don't you have a date with Logan tonight? You have been spending all of your free time with him."

Joy was disappointed that Dymond still seemed to have a problem with her relationship with Logan, but she wasn't giving up on the two of them becoming friends.

"I don't spend all of my free time with him," she corrected. "But Logan has to work tonight. Yet if he didn't, I wanted us to spend some time together. This is something historic with Obama running for president, and it would be unique and nice for us to watch it as a family."

Dymond stood by the doorway and stared at her for a few moments. "Joy, I'm sorry. I can't. Like I said, I have already promised my boss that I would be at work right after my last class. However, I'm excited about going to vote with you this year. This will be the first election that I have ever voted in."

Joy quickly hid her sadness. She was truly looking forward to spending tonight with Dymond. However, she was proud that her sister was taking her new job so seriously.

"Okay, maybe we can do something this weekend," she hopefully suggested. She hadn't seen Dymond much at all this week. It was almost like she was still at *Criswell* instead of being back home.

"Sounds like fun," Dymond smiled. "I don't have to work." Waving goodbye, her sister hurried out of the kitchen and through the front door, closing it softly behind her.

At least Dymond is excited about us doing something together this weekend. Now all I have to do is find a way to make her not dislike Logan so much. Joy knew that was better said than done.

Chapter Nineteen

"I can't believe the captain is making me work all the way out here. I'm well enough to be with Peggy," Logan complained. "Shit, this isn't what I wanted to be doing, or thought I would be doing, when he told me I could come back early. I'm going to have another talk with him as soon as I get back to the station. I can't get pulled off this case."

Logan was going over ways to plead his case inside his head when the sound of a speeding car caught his attention. "What in the hell was that?" he exclaimed as the black BMW sped past his patrol car.

"Oh, that person is going to get a speeding ticket. There was no way they weren't over the speed limit."

Flipping on his siren, Logan left his hiding place behind the trees and drove behind the speeding vehicle. At first, he didn't think the car was going to stop, but it finally pulled over to the side of the road.

Logan got out of his patrol car and made his way slowly over to the driver's door. He knocked on the window and waited for the person to acknowledge him. The window came down slowly as the passenger's head turned and looked at him.

"Yes, Officer? Did I do something wrong?" the young blond girl asked him. "I didn't mean to."

"License and registration," Logan requested.

"Okay, just a minute," she answered.

He waited while the girl got the paperwork he asked for. "Here you go, Officer." The girl handed him the information. "Am I going to get a ticket?"

Logan glanced down at the name on the driver's license and it said Haley Jane. "Miss Jane, you were driving fifty-five mph in a thirty-five mph zone. So, yes you are going to get a speeding ticket."

"Can't you just give me a warning? I'm going to be late for class. Furthermore, I can't afford a ticket," she complained. "I need that money for books. The college I attend is very expensive and I can't afford to waste my money on a dumb ticket."

"I'm sorry ma'am, but I can't help you." Logan filled out the information and tore it off, handing it to the girl in the car.

"Isn't there anything I can do that will make you forget this ever happened?" Haley asked him. "I'm sure a handsome guy like yourself wouldn't mind tearing up that ticket for me."

He couldn't believe this girl was flirting with him to get out of a ticket. Some of the officers back at the station might have fallen for it, but he wasn't one of them. He had written out the ticket and she was going to take it.

"Ma'am, there isn't anything I can do for you. All the information you need is on the ticket. Please take it." Logan waved the ticket at the girl in the car and waited.

"Fine, but I still think it's unfair," she yelled before snatching the ticket and her other information out his hand.

Logan stepped back from the car and watched as the driver pulled out and drove away from him. Shaking his head, he made his way back to his car and got inside. He couldn't believe how people that got caught speeding never thought it was their fault. There were speed limits for a reason, and the more people understand that, the better off they would be.

Taking a quick glance at his watch, he noticed it was time for lunch. Instead of getting something to eat, he was going back to the station. He had a few things to talk over with his captain, and he would check in with Joy. It had been two days since he talked to her, and he was missing her like crazy.

* * * *

Way across town inside the hallway, Haley glanced at the ticket one more time before she shoved it inside her purse. She couldn't believe that cop gave her a ticket after she asked him not to. *What in the hell was wrong with these people here?* Back at home, all she had to do was bat her baby blues, flash a cute smile, and usually most of the cops just let her go with a warning. But not that dumb ass she ran into earlier.

Shit, she didn't have time to be late to this class. It was bad enough the professor was a pain in her ass. Plus, she got seated behind a girl she couldn't stand. All she wanted to do was pass this one class so she would be able to graduate on time and not take summer classes, but it wasn't working out the way she planned. However, she wasn't a quitter, and she was going to do what she had to do. She had plans, and everything was going to work out as she wanted it, come hell or high water.

Chapter Twenty

Brushing her hair off her shoulder, Dymond listened as the professor went over the assignment for her journalism class, but she couldn't keep her mind focused. Why did her sister have to fall for Logan so fast? At first, she was thrilled when Joy told her about her date. However, she never thought Logan would become a permanent part of their lives so fast.

Well, he wasn't really a permanent part, but if she guessed correctly, it wasn't that far away. Things were going fine when it was just the two of them. Logan didn't need to enter into the picture and mess up her perfect family.

Why couldn't Joy understand her dislike for Logan? Sure, he hadn't done anything to her personally, but she wasn't going to let him ruin Joy's life the way her father did her mother's.

Every time Joy talked about their mom, she was happy until Bill Richardson entered it and shattered her heart. After that, she became a different person. All of her attention became 'Bill this' and 'Bill that.' She wouldn't allow Logan to walk in and do that to her sister. It was only fair that she save Joy before she fell under Logan's spell. If that happened, there would be no getting her sister back, and she would truly be alone in the world.

Logan was an attractive guy and was probably used to getting his way all the time with women. Hell, his job made him a woman magnet. Why couldn't Joy see that he wasn't about to be faithful to her. Was it because her sister spent so much time watching over her that her radar might be broken when it came to men like her current boyfriend?

She couldn't and wouldn't let him steal Joy away from her. Her sister was the only family she had left, and she loved her too much to let her get involved with a guy who may not be in love with her. Joy deserved more than that and with her help, her sister would find it. It just wasn't going to be with Logan Scott.

"Excuse me, do you have a pen that I can borrow?" A light tap on her shoulder made Dymond shove her inner thoughts to the back of her mind and glance over her shoulder. She tried not to roll her eyes at the girl sitting behind her. She might have found someone she hated more than Logan Scott.

Haley Jane was a pain in her ass. She was always coming into class late, flirting with the professor, and all the guys in class. Haley reminded her of the girls back at *Criswell,* and she didn't want to be reminded of that time in her life. Honestly, she truly thought Haley was a waste of space, but she couldn't tell her the truth. As hard as it was, she kept her opinion to herself.

"Didn't I give you an ink pen yesterday?" Dymond asked. She was tired of being this girl's supply store. Damn, they were in college now. She wasn't here to take care of Haley. It might make a difference if they were friends, but they weren't, and they would never be. However, she couldn't be nasty, because Joy would think better of her.

"I lost it somewhere," Haley whined, shrugging her shoulder. "Sorry. Can I have another one?"

Picking up an extra pen off the desk, Dymond handed it to Haley and hoped this would be the end of her pushy classmate bothering her. It was beginning to get on her last nerve. "Here you go. Please try to keep up with this one."

"Thanks, Dymond," Haley said, snatching the pen away from her. "You are such a nice person. I knew you wouldn't tell me no. You aren't as bad as I thought you were." Patting her on the shoulder, Haley moved back from her.

Don't let her goad you, Dymond said to herself. She didn't have time to worry about her snobby-ass Reese Witherspoon look-a-like classmate. Honestly, she had more pressing things to attend to like finding a way to get Joy's attention away from Logan and back on her. She would do whatever it took, but she was going to save Joy from herself, even if her sister didn't know she needed to be saved. Her sister had taken care of her for so long and now it was time for her to return the favor.

* * * *

Later that night at work, Dymond glanced up from her homework assignment as the bell went off above the door. Working all these double shifts were getting to her, but the paychecks were well worth it. She watched as two guys, one black and one was white, made their way to the back of the store. They grabbed some junk food off the shelves before making their way back up to her.

They tossed the items on the counter and waited for her to ring them up. From the corner of her eye, Dymond noticed how the black boy kept looking at her. Great, she knew that look. What was he going to say to her?

"Don't I know you? You look very familiar. I know that I have seen you somewhere before."

She shook her head and kept on ringing up the items. "I don't think we know each other," Dymond responded, hoping he would just drop it. She was used to guys using that line on her, and it was getting old.

"Yes, we do," the guy said looking at her even harder.

"Luther, the girl said she doesn't know you. Leave her alone," the blond guy she secretly thought was cute said, cutting in. She had a *huge* weakness for long hair on guys.

"Ridge, shut up," Luther yelled back. "I know who she is now. Dymond Simmons. We almost went to the same high school together until her sister Joy sent her off to boarding school."

Dymond prayed that Luther didn't notice how she did a double take. She couldn't believe that this was the same Luther who was the track star of their town a few years back. She took in his disheveled appearance and wondered what in the hell happened to him.

"Luther, it's so good to see you. Sorry, I didn't recognize you at first."

"Not a problem. We really didn't hang around each other that much. When did you get back from boarding school? Have you already graduated?"

"I got back last month. I talked my sister into letting me finish my last year of college here. *Criswell* was more like an all girls school instead of a boarding school, in my opinion, since there weren't any hot guys there," she complained. "I couldn't take being there anymore."

"Are you going to hog all of this gorgeous girl's time or will you finally introduce me? You know I have such a weakness for a stunning face," Ridge interrupted and winked at her.

"Ridge, this is Dymond Simmons. Dymond, this is my buddy Ridge, but don't let him charm you," Luther said, hurrying through the introductions.

"Why shouldn't I let you charm me?" she asked Ridge, staring into his gorgeous blue-green eyes.

"Well...I have been told that I'm a bad boy," Ridge answered.

"Oh, I love bad boys. I find them very exciting."

"Have you ever dated a boy as bad as me?"

"How bad are you?" Dymond tossed back, enjoying their verbal game.

"I guess we might have to go out on a date for you to find out."

"I guess we will."

"How much is our stuff?" Ridge asked.

She had forgotten all about their food. Dymond quickly finished ringing up the stuff. "It's $12.75."

Ridge tossed a fifty dollar bill down on the counter. "Don't worry about the change. You can keep it. Come on, man, let's go." Grabbing the stuff off the counter, Ridge gave her one more look before he left with Luther following behind him.

"Wow, he was hot!" Dymond gushed as she leaned over the counter. "I hope he comes in here again." Joy would have a fit if she knew she was flirting with a total stranger at her job, but what her sister didn't know wouldn't hurt her.

Chapter Twenty-One

"How was your day?" a warm breath asked against her ear as strong fingers massaged the stiffness from the back of her neck. "I've missed you."

I could get used to this, Joy thought as Logan's hands moved from her neck and wrapped around her waist. Having a man in her life that focused his attention on her and wondered about her day instead of just wanting her to listen about his was something she had been waiting for most of her life.

"I missed you, too. I wanted to call you, but work kept me so busy that when I got home, all I could do was just hit the bed. Is there any way I can make it up to you?"

A gasp flew from Joy's lips as Logan spun her around and yanked her against his chest. "I can suggest anything I want to you, and you'll do it?" The hope in his voice made her wished she had asked this question earlier.

Laughing, Joy wrapped her arms around Logan's neck. The harder she tried to move things slowly between them, it just wasn't working. It shouldn't have come as a surprise to her, because Logan had drawn her attention from the very beginning. They were reaching a point in their relationship were things were becoming more involved, and she loved it.

"Depends on what you want, handsome," she flirted back.

"Spend the night with me. Neither one of us has to work tomorrow. I want to wake up with you in my arms."

Spend the night?

It would be amazing to wake up in Logan's arms. God, his every movement reminded her of his sexual attractiveness. A part of her wondered how many other women he had made this tempting offer to.

"I don't know. Are you sure we are at that step yet?" she teased, shoving her own pessimistic thoughts away.

"Joy, I want to make love to you. However, if you aren't ready, I'm more than willing to just fall asleep with you next to me. I only want to spend this time with you without any kind of interruptions."

Why was she stalling so damn much? Logan was freaking sexy in so many ways. Her body ached for his touch, and more than once she had dreamt about being crushed against his hard chest. She was tired of fighting her devastating need to be close to him.

"Yes, I would love to spend the night with you...but..." her voice trailed off as she thought about something.

Logan's hands eased down her back and grabbed her butt. "How about we stop worrying about the future and just do it. We can deal with anything that might happen later." What he said was so sensible. Why worry about the future when this perfect moment was right here in front of her?

"You're right," she agreed, working on the front button on Logan's shirt. Pushing it open, she ran her fingers through his thick chest hair. "God, you're so hot!"

Sure, she had seen Logan shirtless before, but this time was different. They were going to make love for the first time.

"You don't look so bad yourself," Logan said as he worked on the buttons on the back of her sweater. Slipping it down her arms, he dropped it on the floor next to their feet.

"Your breasts are so beautiful." Taking the palms of his hands, Logan ran them along the sides of her swollen breast, then paused to slightly pinch her hard nipples.

"Oh, that feels so good," Joy moaned as she swayed in the circle of Logan's embrace.

"Brown eyes, it's only going to get better." A second later, she was swept up in Logan's arms as he carried her toward his bedroom.

* * * *

Logan was trying his best to move slowly, but the feel of Joy's silky skin was driving him to the point of no return. He wasn't used to moving at this pace with any woman, but Joy was special. He wanted to know what was going on in her heart and mind before he got to sample her luscious body.

In the past, he wasn't big on relationships because of the dangers that came along with his job. He couldn't let a woman become emotionally attracted or involved with him. He didn't want her to be worried about him. However, Joy was unique. He wanted her to be thinking about him, because he sure in the hell thought about her every minute of the day.

Joy truly didn't understand that he was always in a semi-aroused state anytime he was around her. The only thing that kept him from tossing her over his shoulder and having his way was Joy. She deserved romance and a man who wanted to listen to her problems.

"I'm going to cherish every inch of your gorgeous body," he told Joy as he laid her down on his bed. "After tonight, you're going to know how much you mean to me."

Leaning back on her elbows, Joy looked at him from underneath her thick eyelashes. "You say a lot. How do I know you're going to live up to it?"

Oh, she wanted to test him?

Logan quickly removed his shoes and pants so he was only clad in his black boxers that were barely containing his raging erection. He couldn't just have his way with Joy the way he was dying to. He would move slowly and ease his way into her heart. He wasn't positive if she had been hurt by love or was just afraid to be in it, but he wasn't going to give up on her.

"Come here, Joy. I want to show you how much I want you."

Sliding off the bed, Joy walked toward him and stopped within touching distance. Her soft brown eyes stared into his like she trusted him with her life, and that endearing look touched the deepest part of his soul. He didn't want to rush the beauty of the moment, so he stood there drinking in the sight of Joy's beautiful breasts.

"Is there something wrong?" Joy asked when he continued to stare at her. She started to cover them up, but he brushed her hands out of the way. "Don't cover up perfection. I want to look at you. I've never seen a more gorgeous sight." Lifting her hands, he cupped one of her breasts as he lowered his mouth and sucked at the other distended nipple.

Joy cried out at the sensation of her nipple inside Logan's scorching mouth. The invigorating feeling sent a pool of moisture into her panties and down her legs.

"Do you like this, brown eyes?" Logan asked as he let go of her breasts and unbuttoned her skirt. He pushed it down her hips and helped her out of it.

"Are you wet for me? If I stick my hand in that scrap of fabric you call underwear, will my fingers get soaked?" Without waiting for a reply, he promptly moved his hand and rewarded her with a smug grin. "I love that I know you so well." Taking his middle finger, he worked it into her tight warmth.

"Mmmm," Joy moaned as she dropped her head on his chest. "That feels *so* good."

Joy didn't have time to utter another word before Logan kissed her. No wait...he wasn't kissing her, but making love to her mouth. He licked and nibbled at her bottom lip like it was the best delicacy he had ever had the honor to sample.

Lord, it felt like he was making her toes curl into his thick carpet. Shit, this man was just too dangerous. How could he make a simple kiss seem better than the act of making love?

Wait...Maybe not better, her mind corrected but pretty freaking close, in her modest opinion.

Logan sucked at her lips for a few more seconds before he let them go and reluctantly removed his hand from her body. "How about we remove these and get more comfortable?" he asked, tugging at the side of her underwear. "I'm so ready to make love to you that I'm about to explode."

Joy paused as she looked into Logan's desire-filled gaze. This had to be a dream. No man could be this romantic, hot, caring, and understanding all at the same time. She wasn't lucky enough to get a man with all of these qualities, but she was going to live in this fantasy world as long as she could.

"Do it," she whispered softly. She stood still as Logan eased her drenched panties down her legs and tossed them away.

"You smell delicious," he moaned as he ran his knuckles over her damp curls. "I can't wait until I'm buried deep inside of you."

"I can't wait either," Joy exclaimed as he stood up and swept her back into his arms.

Logan tenderly placed Joy down on the bed before lying next to her. "You have the most beautiful skin I have ever seen. It's so rich, silky, and brown. I could touch you all day and never get tired."

Joy felt her cheeks get hot at Logan's flattering remarks as he licked at the side of her neck. She was glad that he couldn't see how much his words meant to her. He might think she wasn't used to getting compliments. She wasn't, but he didn't need to know that. Closing her eyes, she relaxed her body and got lost in Logan's lovemaking, blocking everything else out.

She was so lost in what he was doing to her that she wasn't aware Logan had moved until the cool air hit her body. Opening her eyes, she stared at Logan as he removed his boxers and his thick, beautiful erection sprang free. She wasn't allowed a lot of time to appreciate it, because Logan quickly put on a condom and covered her body.

"Baby, are you ready?" his deep voice inquired as he eased her thighs apart with his knee. "I'm about ready to die here if I don't get into you soon."

"I'm ready for anything you want to give me," Joy tossed back. She was tired of living for everyone else. Tonight was about her and no one else.

"Slow and sweet or fast and hard?" The question was asked in a low heat filled voice.

The tip of Logan's erection was posed at her entrance and Joy couldn't think straight at all. "What?" she asked locking eyes with Logan. God, why was he asking so many questions at a time like this?

"How do you want it? Slow and sweet or fast and hard," he asked again, pushing his hard cock a little further into her heat.

"Surprise me."

Grabbing her wrists, Logan pulled her arms above her head and he entered her with one sure thrust, making her gasp from shock and incredible pleasure.

Chapter Twenty-Two

He covered her body with his chest and started pumping in and out of her at the pace that was making the headboard thump against the wall behind them. Logan knew he had never been inside a woman this tight before. Suddenly, Joy wrapped her legs around his hips, pulling him even deeper inside of her warm, snug heat.

"Oh, my God! What are you doing to me?" she panted as her short nails raked down his back.

The sudden pain only enhanced the pleasure of the moment. It didn't make him want to stop. *Hell*, he wanted to keep going so he could make her do it again.

"I guess you like what I'm doing to this hot, little body of yours?" Logan asked as he unwrapped Joy's legs from his waist and placed them on his shoulders. "I'm going to keep this up until you realize that you're mine. I don't share, and it will be a cold day in hell before I ever think about letting you go."

"Ooooh…mmmm," she groaned low in her throat as he sped up his pace. "That feels so good."

"Am I hitting your spot, brown eyes?"

"Yes," Joy moaned as her eyes started to close from pleasure. "You're finding it so perfectly."

Hell…Yeah, I am, Logan thought.

He was finding it so fucking wonderfully that Joy wasn't going to think about another man after this. He was proving to her just how first-rate things could be between the two of them. Turning his head, he kissed the side of

Joy's legs, falling more in love with the softness of her body. It wasn't right for one woman to feel this fine.

It went on and on for so long that Logan just got lost in the incredulity at how Joy could keep up with him. He had a strong sexual appetite, and his past girlfriends *never* liked this position. He always thought it was him, and now he knew it was them. They weren't as sexually adept as Joy.

"Logan, it's about to happen," Joy purred as her wet muscles tightened around his cock.

Shit, he wasn't far behind her, either. Only a few more thrust, and he'll be there, too. Damn it. Joy was going to kill him, and he loved every minute of it. This was the best night of his life, and it was only going to get better.

"Let it happen, brown eyes. I want to hear what I do to you. Scream for me."

"Looogan," Joy screamed as her orgasm raked through her body.

Gripping Joy's hips harder, Logan kept pushing forward until the recognizable feelings started coming over his entire body. He threw his head back and yelled Joy's name at his release until he couldn't do it anymore. As his heart rate slowed and got back down to normal, he gently removed Joy's legs from his shoulders and withdrew from her.

"Are you okay?" he asked as he made quick work with the condom by tossing it in the trashcan next to his bed. He was too tired to even get up. Besides, he wasn't ready to leave Joy.

"That was incredible," Joy whispered, cuddling up next to him. "I don't think it can get any better than that."

Was she sending him out a challenge?

"Honey, I think I might have to prove you wrong," Logan chuckled as he pulled her damp body even closer to his sweaty one. "However, I think we should get some sleep so we'll have energy for later."

"Are you saying you aren't strong enough to go another round right now?" she teased, running her finger through his chest hair.

"I'm not saying that," Logan answered as he covered their bodies with a sheet. "I only want you to be well rested so when we make love again, I can have your full attention." He gathered Joy close to his heart and held her until they both fell asleep.

Chapter Twenty-Three

"Do you really have to leave?" the soft feminine voice whispered while trailing kisses down the lower part of his back. "I thought we were going to spend the day getting to know each other, making love and having fun."

Logan hated leaving Joy, but he was needed at the station. New information. A good solid lead had come in this time, and he wasn't going to miss being a part of it. He was glad Peggy had called him, but he was pissed it meant he was leaving Joy all warm and sexy in his bed.

"Sweetheart, I would love to stay here with you, but I can't. I swear I'll make it up to you." Looking over his shoulder, Logan winked then smiled at Joy before getting up off the bed. "You're more than welcome to stay here. I would love to come home and find you naked waiting for me in bed. Hell, that's every guy's fantasy, having a hot woman in his bed.

Shaking her head, Joy got out of the rumpled bed, pulling the sheet with her. He loved her modesty. It was so sweet. After everything they did last night, she was still shy about showing off her body in daylight. He was going to find a way to make that happen. Joy had a gorgeous body and shouldn't have to hide it from him.

"No, I should go home. I have to make sure Dymond didn't destroy the house while I was gone."

"Do you think she would do that?" Logan asked as he strolled toward his closet.

"I'm positive that she didn't. Dymond isn't like that. She has a wild streak sometimes, and I think she likes to test my patience, but she would never do anything to make me not trust her."

Finding what clothes she could in his bedroom, Joy got dressed. "I'm going into the living room to find the rest of my clothes."

Logan eyed Joy's bare breasts and felt his morning erection get even harder. Shit, why didn't he take her up on her offer earlier for a little fun?

"Do you need me to help you look?"

Joy laughed softly and shook her head. "I believe I know what my own clothes look like." The beginning of a smile tipped the corners of her full lips. She glanced down at his erection before leaving the room.

"Did she really think I wasn't going to take her up on her sexy offer?" Logan said under his breath as he followed Joy out of his bedroom door. Easing up behind her, he slipped his arms around her waist.

"Logan, what are you doing?" Joy shrieked, moving around, trying to get out of his light hold.

"I'm taking you up on your offer." He didn't allow Joy a chance to reply before he took her over to the couch. Sitting down, he pulled her between his legs and made fast work of her underwear. Logan lifted Joy above his throbbing erection and entered her with one fast thrust.

"Shit, baby," he moaned as Joy's body welcomed his. Logan thought she felt so fantastic as his hands just held her hips in place so she wouldn't be able to move. He wanted to enjoy the moment while it lasted. Pulling her torso forward, Logan licked at her perky nipples before easing one into his mouth.

"Oh, Logan," Joy murmured as her hips started moving up and down. "That feels so unbelievable."

Letting go of Joy's nipple, Logan glanced down watching as his erection went in and out of her wetness underneath her skirt. The sight of their different colors turned him on even more. If he wasn't horny before, he was over the edge now.

He wanted to go slow. He honestly did, but Joy just felt so right and good. Today was better than last night. He would have bet a million dollars it wouldn't have been possible and lost. He wasn't going to give Joy up for anything in the world. She was his, and if she wasn't aware of it, she would be before the day was over.

Logan slid his hands underneath Joy's short flirty skirt and held her bare ass in his palms, meeting her thrust for thrust. "You're mine," he growled deep in his throat. "Say it."

Dark brown eyes connected with his, and Joy shook her head. "No."

"I'm serious. Say you're mine."

"I won't do it," she tossed back as she bounced her perfect body against his thighs.

The sound of their wet bodies slapping together echoed in the room, making Logan want to find his release soon, but he couldn't until Joy admitted what he needed to hear.

Holding her still so she couldn't move, Logan watched Joy for a few minutes to see if what he was doing was finally setting in. "Answer me."

"Let me go. I need..." she whimpered trying to move her hips.

"What do you need baby?"

"You know."

"No, I don't. Why don't you tell me?"

"I want you to move," Joy answered, wiggling her lower body the best she could in his firm grip.

Logan sucked in a breath between his teeth. Joy was killing him without her even knowing it. However, he was going to see this out. Besides, who said that he couldn't have a little fun with his sex?

"Oh, you mean like this?" He lifted Joy up and brought her back down inch by inch over his erection.

"Yes, but faster," she panted.

"I wish I could help you, but I can't until I hear the words. Are you willing to tell me the words?"

Biting her plump bottom lip, Joy shook her head. He loved how her mind and body were at odds with each other. The battle of wills between them was a turn-on. "Let me see if I can help you with that."

Once again, he raised Joy back up over his cock until only the tip was left in her and then slowly fed her the rest of him until her tight ass rested against his thighs again. He *loved* the way her breasts bounced with each movement. There wasn't a sexier sight than a woman's bare breasts in his opinion.

"Please stop teasing me," Joy begged, grabbing his arms. "I can't take much more."

"You know how to make it end," he taunted, softly. "Say you're mine, and I'll give you the orgasm your body is screaming for."

"Logan, you aren't playing fair."

"Honey, I never said I was a fair man," Logan tossed back as he picked up Joy for the last time, he hoped. The slickness of her body was coating his cock, and he was barely holding on to his thread of control. His game of trying to break Joy was beginning to backfire on him.

"God, I'm yours!" Joy shouted. "Please, don't tease me anymore. I can't take it. I'm dying to come."

"FINALLY!" Logan growled deep in his throat as he thrust deep into Joy. They screamed in unison as their releases hit them.

* * * *

Logan wrapped his arms around Joy and took a deep breath, trying to slow down his pounding heart. It had never, and he truly meant never, been this good with other women. Joy was unique and all his.

He felt Joy's body shaking against his, and it sent him into immediate panic. Was she crying? Had be gotten too rough with her? God, what if he had messed things up between them? He would fix it. He couldn't and wouldn't lose her.

"Brown eyes, are you okay? Did I hurt you?" Moving Joy away from him, he was shocked to see that she wasn't crying, but laughing.

"What's so funny?" he frowned.

"You're so late for work now. What is going to be your excuse? 'Sorry, Captain that I'm late, but I was craving a little chocolate this morning'?"

Logan honestly tried not to laugh, but he couldn't hold it in. He threw back his head and let out a deep, gut-wrenching laugh. "Okay, Miss Simmons. I really do need to get to work. As you just pointed out to me, I'm beyond late because of you." He lifted Joy off his softening erection and stood her in front of him. "I'm going to take a shower. Do you want to join me?" Logan asked, running his hands over her breasts.

"A shower and nothing else? I need to get home."

He held up two fingers. "Scouts honor. Nothing else will happen."

"Great. Let's go." Joy stripped out of her skirt, left it on the floor, and headed for his bedroom.

"I'm so glad that I was never in the boy scouts," Logan said under his breath, dropping his hand as he followed Joy out of the room.

Chapter Twenty-Four

For the second time that month, the woman knelt down in front of the grave and brushed the dirt off the marble headstone with the palm of her hand. She wanted to come more often, but it just wasn't possible with everything going on. She had to get her plan started and underway so it would be perfect in the end. No one suspected anything was going on, and that is the way she wanted it to be.

"Hey, I had to come and see you today. You would be so proud of me. Everything is going to plan. I'm getting myself more and more involved with the people who hurt you. They are so incredibly stupid. I'm fitting right in with them, and no one knows who I am."

"It sickens me to see how they have all went on with their lives without giving you a second thought. Those people in that town act like they have nothing to be sorry for at all, but I won't let them forget your name. I'll make sure when all of this is done and over, you'll get the respect that you deserve."

* * * *

Unlocking the front door, Joy walked inside her house; she tossed the keys on the table next to the door and closed it behind her. She felt amazing after spending the night with Logan. He made her experience things that she had long thought had died in her. This was the first time in a long time she would have a boyfriend for the holidays.

If everything went okay, she might even have someone for Valentine's Day, but she wasn't going to jump that far ahead with their relationship. She was going to take it one day at a time. Besides, she had something to discuss with Dymond first, and she prayed her sister wouldn't give her any problems.

"Dymond, are you home?" she yelled, walking through the living room.

"I'm in the kitchen," her sister yelled back.

Going back to the kitchen, Joy stopped in the doorway when her eyes landed on a guy sitting at the table with her sister. Who in the world was he and why was he in her house?

"Dymond, are you going to introduce me to your guest?"

Dymond's eyes darted nervously back and forth between her and the guy at the table. It was like her sister wasn't expecting her to be back home yet.

"Joy, this is Ridge. I met him at work. He just came over to talk," Dymond said. "Ridge, this is my sister, Joy."

"Nice to meet you, Ridge," Joy said, walking into the kitchen and stopping by the edge of the table.

"You, too, Miss Simmons," Ridge smiled, standing up. "I guess I better go. I need to take care of some things."

Joy noticed how Ridge's blue-green eyes were very cold, despite the smile he was trying to give her. There was something not right about him, but she couldn't put her finger on it. She wouldn't get into it while he was here. However, after he was gone, she was going to have a discussion with Dymond.

"You don't have to leave on my account," Joy said.

"No, I need to go. Thanks for inviting me over, Dymond." Ridge stepped around her and practically ran out of the room for the front door.

"Wait, let me walk you out." Dymond brushed past her hurrying after her guest.

Falling down in the seat Ridge just vacated, Joy massaged her temples as she waited for Dymond to come back. What was her sister doing bringing someone home she met at her job? She knew nothing about Ridge at all. Now he knew where they lived and could come back and do anything he wanted to them.

"I know you're pissed about finding him here with me. Ridge is just a friend. Nothing else. I'm not planning on sleeping with him. I don't want a lecture from you about him. Not with you spending the night with Logan," Dymond tossed out, standing inside the entranceway.

"Don't you dare start yelling at me," Joy snapped, dropping her hand. "Come in here and have a seat. We have a lot of stuff to talk about."

Dymond came into the kitchen and sat down across from her. She had to approach this the right way with her sister since her dislike for Logan was so strong. They hadn't lived together in a while, and she wanted things to work out between them.

"Dymond, I'm not upset that Ridge was in the house. Of course, you can have friends come over to visit you. I like that you're making new friends, but was it truly wise to invite someone in our house that you barely know?"

"You barely knew Logan, and I caught the two of you going at it right in this room like a couple of rabbits."

No, she didn't say that to me, Joy thought glaring at her sister. Calm down. Don't get into an argument with her. That is what she wants you to do.

"Okay, you're right. Logan and I were in here kissing, but I have the right to do that. I'm an adult." Joy held up her hand, cutting off Dymond from speaking. "I'm not saying you aren't an adult. I'm only implying you shouldn't have invited a total stranger to our home. It wasn't safe."

"How do you know that Logan is so safe?" Dymond demanded, tossing her long hair over her shoulders in a gesture of defiance.

Joy remembered how her sister always loved doing that move when she was a little girl and didn't get her way. She laughed silently at the memory.

"Dymond, I didn't know that Logan was safe. That's why I met him for our first date. I was testing the waters with him. It's something every woman should do. I'm only trying to help you make good choices in life. You might hate me for it, but I'm not going to stop because of the fact you drive me up the wall. I love you."

"Fine. I'll make sure the next time I meet Ridge, it won't be at the house," Dymond replied in a rush of words. "What else do you want to talk about? I know there's something else."

Here goes nothing.

"I was wondering what would you think about Logan spending Thanksgiving with us. I wasn't going to ask him until I discussed it with you first."

Her sister's mouth dropped open like she couldn't believe what she had just asked her. Dymond's astonishment was obviously genuine, and she regretted asking the question now.

"You want Logan to spend the entire day with us?"

"No. I would like for him to stop by after dinner. I'm not positive he will be able to do it or not. He might be working or spending the day with his family."

"Go ahead and ask him over. I want to get to know the guy that has my sister all crazy in love."

"I'm not crazy in love," Joy denied.

"If you say so," Dymond snickered, getting up from the chair. "I'm going to change and meet some of my friends. We are going to study for a test. I'll be home late since I don't have class or work tomorrow."

"Have fun with your friends."

"I will," Dymond yelled back at her as she left the kitchen.

After Dymond had left to meet her friends, Joy was still sitting inside the chair, glad that everything had worked out with their conversation. Maybe her sister was starting to see Logan wasn't a threat to their relationship after all. She wanted to be totally happy with today's events, but she couldn't quite get there.

Ridge was still setting off her big sister radar in a huge way. There was something not right about him, and she couldn't put her finger on it. When she got a chance, she would bring up Dymond's new interest to Logan. He might be able to help her out.

Chapter Twenty-Five

The next day, Joy wrapped the heavy coat around her body some more, trying to block out the cold as she stood out in the line, but it would be worth it. Anyway, there weren't that many people in front of her. Before long, she would be able get inside of the building and cast her vote. It was so worth battling the cold to be able to do this today, and having Dymond next to her only made it more special.

"I'm so proud of you for getting up early and coming with me this morning. You will never forget this. Just think, you'll be able to tell your kids that you made a piece of history happen."

Dymond pulled the black hoodie down further on her head and glanced over at her. "I wasn't going to miss doing this today with you," her sister replied. "I don't get excited about a lot of stuff, but I'm really excited about doing this. We're going to make history together."

Joy shoved her hands into the pockets of her leather jacket to keep them warm as they moved forward when the couple in front of them stepped up. She wasn't going to bring it up to Dymond, because her sister usually got upset when she talked about their mother. However, she secretly wished their mother was still alive and able to vote today.

Danielle Simmons worked so hard to make her and Dymond's life so much better. This moment would have been so important to her. That's one of the main reasons she wanted to get her vote in today. She was doing it out of respect for her mother. In addition, she honestly thought that Senator Obama would make an amazing president. The world was ready for change, and he was the man that was going to bring it.

"Hey, what are you in such deep thought about?" Dymond asked. "I've been talking to you for the past five minutes and you haven't answered me."

"I was just thinking about some stuff," Joy answered.

"Like what?"

"Nothing important," Joy exclaimed, studying Dymond.

"Are you sure that you weren't thinking about Ridge? It's not like you just to let something like that drop. I know you still aren't happy with me hanging out with him."

"Dymond, I only meet Ridge yesterday, but I don't get a good feeling about him. I think you should try to distance yourself from him. I know there has to be a better quality of guys at your college for you to date. I know *nothing* about this guy. I only want the best for you."

"I'm not getting into this with you. I'm smart enough to make my own decisions. Ridge is just a friend, and you're reading too much into it. Stop trying to control my life and just live yours with Logan. I know that is what you really want to do, anyway."

Joy was stunned to hear Dymond talk like this. Where in the world did Dymond think she didn't want her around now since she was dating Logan? It wasn't true at all.

"Dymond, you have it all wrong. Logan isn't going to replace you in my life. You're my sister and I love you. You know that, don't you?"

"I know you do, but..."

"But what...tell me," Joy insisted. She was stunned that Dymond thought she was going to dump her because of Logan. They were family, and nothing was more important than family.

"Dymond, talk to me. I want to understand what's going on with you." This was the first time in a long time her sister had opened up to her. She wanted to get as much as she could out in the open while Dymond was being so responsive.

Shaking her head, Dymond moved away from her. "That's okay. I'm just running my mouth, and I should have kept quiet. I'm fine. I shouldn't have said anything to you. Logan is great for you. I have never seen you look happier."

Joy wanted to continue this conversation so bad, but she could tell Dymond was done, so she let it go for now. However, she was going to find a way to get the truth out of Dymond. There was something deeper going on here, but she just didn't know what it was.

One way or another, Dymond was going to reveal her true feelings about Logan. Because if she kept it bottled up like this, things were going to explode, and she didn't want that to happen. The two most important people in her life didn't need to hate each other.

Chapter Twenty-Six

"Are you proud that you voted?" Joy asked Dymond as she watched Katie Couric announce Senator Barack Obama as the 44th President Elect of the United States. "I think this memory will stay with me forever."

"Yeah, it is pretty cool to be here with you like this and seeing all of this happen. I'm glad you are here with me and not over at Logan's house."

The dislike in Dymond's voice rang through the house, and Joy wanted to get to the bottom of it. She respected Dymond's earlier request to leave it alone, but she wasn't going to do it now. She would find out why her boyfriend was on her sister's most hated list.

"Once and for all, what is your problem with Logan?" Joy asked. "Please tell me. I want to know so I can help you move past it. I hate not being able to invite Logan over because you hate him so much."

Glancing away from the television, Dymond tossed her a look. "What makes Logan so special? You act like he's the best thing in the world. Don't you even think for a moment you could be wrong about him? What if he breaks your heart and just walks away? How will you deal with it?"

The way the questions were thrown at her took Joy back a little. She wasn't prepared for them at all. Dymond had really given her relationship with Logan a lot of thought and drawn her own conclusions about him.

"Dymond, Logan is the kind of man that I have been looking for. He's warm, sweet, and understanding. I don't think he's the best thing in the world, but I do think he's a wonderful man. I'm not thinking about Logan breaking my heart. But if it does happen, I'll deal with it and go on."

"Yeah, sure you will," Dymond snapped getting up from the couch. "I'm going out for a while. I need some fresh air." Grabbing her coat out of the closet, her sister headed for the front door.

"How long are you going to be gone?"

"I don't know, but I'll be back home later on tonight. Why don't you call Logan over while I'm gone since you can't do it with me here?" Opening the front door, Dymond went out, slamming it behind her.

Chapter Twenty-Seven

"I don't know where I'm going wrong with her. I believe she hates me." After thinking about it for over an hour, Joy finally decided to call Logan to see if he could come by for a little while. She needed someone to talk to and he was the best person.

"Dymond doesn't hate you. She loves you. That's why she's so upset at the sudden appearance of me in your life. She was used to it just being the two of you for so long and now it's something different. No matter how mature Dymond tries to act, she's still young and wants your approval. She might not say it to you, but she does," Logan said, rubbing his hand up and down her denim-clad thigh.

"She doesn't want you to be hurt and she trying to make sure that doesn't happen. I think that shows the sisterly bond she has with you. You should be proud of her. I'm very protective of my siblings, too. So, I understand where Dymond is coming from."

Leaning away from Logan's chest, Joy stared at him. "Do you think that is the reason Dymond's acting out? She thinks I'm not proud of her?"

"No, honey," Logan replied. "I think Dymond is just acting her age. My sister gave my parents hell when she was twenty. It will pass."

"I hope so. I miss the closeness we used to have. I don't want her finding it with other people and start making bad decisions again. She has been so much better lately."

"Are you saying she is hanging out with the wrong crowd? Do you want me to check certain people out for you? I'm busy with my current case, but I don't mind doing a background check. Just give me a name, and I'll find out what I can."

"You would do that for me?" Joy asked, stunned.

"Joy, I'm beginning to have deep feelings for you. So, baby, your problems are my problems. I hate seeing you upset like this."

Should she tell Logan about Ridge? Would getting Logan involved prove Dymond's point in all the ways that mattered? That he was coming into their lives to take over and shove her to the side? No, she wouldn't do it. Instead, she would have another talk with Dymond. They would be able to work things out themselves.

"No, I can take care of this. I don't want to get you involved in my family problems, but I do have a question for you."

Sitting up on the couch, Joy slid her legs underneath her getting more comfortable on the plush cushions. "I want to know what you're doing for Thanksgiving."

"Are you going to invite me over for Thanksgiving dinner?" Logan asked, running his finger down the side of her cheek.

"I was hoping you could come over for dessert. I know you probably want to spend the first part of the day with your family, and I understand that."

"I would love to have a slice of pumpkin or pecan pie with you for Thanksgiving. Is this all right with Dymond? I know we aren't the best of friends yet. I want to spend part of the day with you, but not if it will make it worse for her."

The compassion Logan was showing toward Dymond was tugging at her heart-strings. She really had a winner here, and she wasn't about to lose him. How many guys would be worrying about her sister's feelings instead of their own? Logan was definitely a keeper.

"You're welcome at our house for Thanksgiving. So does that mean I'm going to get a yes?" she questioned, hopefully.

"I'll be here around three o'clock. If I leave my sister's house earlier than that, she would have a fit. Thanksgiving is her holiday. She loves for the family to pile up at her house and enjoy the day. Plus, this year I have to tell everyone about my gorgeous girlfriend. I know they will have twenty questions that I'll have to answer before I get out of there."

"Oh, what are you going to tell them about me?"

"That you're gorgeous, sweet, and I wouldn't know what I would do without you in my life. So, how's that?"

"Three o'clock is fine with me. I'll be waiting for you to show up. Don't you dare disappoint me, especially after all of those wonderful things you just said," Joy teased, poking Logan in the chest with her finger.

"When have I ever disappointed you, brown eyes?" Logan asked as he pulled her across the couch and against his chest.

"So far, I can't say that you have."

"That's right and I plan to keep it that away." Tilting her chin up with his finger, Logan stared into her eyes before capturing her mouth in a slow, wet kiss.

* * * *

Ridge ran his hand across the smooth back of the body lying in bed next to him. It was getting harder and harder to find places to hide out with cops breathing down his neck and knocking on every fucking door of every house in town. In addition, Luther used to be so good at having his back. But over the past few weeks, his buddy was showing up less and less. He didn't know what was going on, but he was going to find out and deal with it. Luther wasn't about to bail on him now.

It would be a cold day in hell before he went down for shooting those two cops by himself. Luther was a part of it just as much as he was. Who gives a damn if he wasn't the one who pulled the trigger?

"What are you thinking about? Your attention sure isn't on me. You know how much I hate that."

Glancing down into a pair of cold blue eyes, Ridge said, "I'm not thinking about anything, Haley. You worry way too much."

"Come on, Ridge. I know you're up to something. Tell me what it is. Or are you thinking about Dymond? I just told you to show that bitch a little attention, not fall for her."

Removing his hand from Haley's back, Ridge fanned his fingers through his hair. He was trying to keep a lot of things going on, and he didn't need Haley's clingy personality. They were only sleeping together and that was it. Haley had no business asking about anything else going on in his life.

"Haley, why don't you worry about yourself and not me? You can't tell me what to do. Why in the hell do you think you can?" Ridge tossed the covers off his body and got out of the bed. Picking up his clothes off the floor, he hurried and got dressed. He quickly found Haley's clothes and tossed them to her. "Get dressed, and get the hell out of here."

"Why are you being such a bastard?" Haley yelled, snatching her jeans and sweater off the bed. "I thought I might be able to spend the night. I wasn't ready to go back home."

"When have you ever spent the night with me?" Ridge asked, watching as Haley put her clothes back on. "You know your place and I suggest you stay in it. We have a good thing going on. I don't want it to be ruined."

Haley's blue eyes turned even colder as she came toward him. Shit, he didn't want to deal with her drama tonight. He just wanted her gone before she pissed him off even more.

"What in the hell are you really up to? I thought you were my boyfriend. I should be able to stay here as long as I want. Don't make me mad. I would hate to give the cops an anonymous tip about where you have been hiding. I think I heard about a nice size reward for your capture. I could always use a little extra money with the Christmas holiday coming up. I have kept my mouth quiet this long about us, but I wouldn't mind telling our little secret now for the right price."

Ridge closed the distance between him and Haley. Grabbing her by the upper arm, he jerked her against his body. "Don't you ever threaten me. Do you understand me?" He tightened his grip making Haley wince. "I'm not a guy you want to mess with. Are we clear with each other?"

"Let go of me. I'm not scared of you," Haley snapped, struggling against his hold.

"See…that's your problem. You need to be scared of me. I'm not one of those guys at your college. When I say something, I mean it. Now, get the rest of your shit and leave!" Ridge flung Haley away from his body and stormed over to the front door. He was about to open it when someone knocked on it.

"Who in the hell is that?' Haley asked.

"I don't know. Who else did you tell about my hideout?"

"No one."

The knock came again followed by a female voice. "Ridge, are you there? It's me, Dymond."

Chapter Twenty-Eight

"Dymond, what are you doing here?" Ridge asked, shutting the door. He glanced back over his shoulder at his closed bedroom door. He hoped Haley stayed in there. He didn't have time to break up a cat fight because Dymond and Haley hated each other.

"You told me I could come by anytime I needed to talk. Should I have not come by?"

Shit, he had forgotten all about that. This is what he gets for thinking with the wrong head. If he didn't want to get Dymond into his bed so bad, he wouldn't have given her his address.

"No, I'm glad you came by," Ridge lied. "What's up?" He was going to think of this as a good thing. Maybe this little chat would give him a better chance at getting Dymond to give him something. He had wanted a taste of her since he laid eyes on her. Her body was killer, and he was dying for a sample.

"My sister is dating this guy and I can't stand him. She thinks he is all she has ever wanted and he isn't," Dymond complained, pacing back and forth in front of him.

"Dymond, why don't you sit down?" Ridge took a seat on the couch and touched the spot next to him. "I can't concentrate with you moving around like that." Besides he wanted to be able to ogle her body at a better angle.

"Fine," Dymond sighed, falling down next to him. "But it isn't going to help. I have to deal with this jerk, and

I hate it. I know he really doesn't love my sister and Joy doesn't see it."

Fuck! Why would Dymond think he would care about anything going on in her sister's life? She meant nothing to him. He was more interested in why she actually showed up at his hideout. Was Dymond really so caught up with her sister's life that she didn't know about him? This was *so* working in his favor. Dymond was desperate for a shoulder to cry on, and he had two to offer up. He could pretend to be understanding to get what he really craved.

"What is your deal about this guy? Did he say something to you?"

"I wish it was that easy, but it isn't. Logan is the perfect man. He's has everything going for him."

Sitting up straighter on the couch, Ridge eyed Dymond. No, his luck wouldn't be this fucking bad. He wasn't going to panic. There were a lot of guys out there with the name Logan.

"Logan. That's your sister's boyfriend's name?" Ridge asked cautiously.

"It's Logan Scott and here's the best part. He's a cop."

Jumping up from the couch, Ridge grabbed Dymond by the arm and dragged her toward the door. "You have to go. I forgot I have to meet someone." He opened the door, shoved Dymond out, and slammed it shut in her shocked face.

"Son of a bitch," he yelled, running his fingers through his hair. How could he be dumb enough to pick a girl whose sister was dating the cop looking for him? All Dymond had to do was mention his name around Logan and he would be in handcuffs. He needed another place to hide and the sooner the better.

Wait! Haley would be able to help him. She found him this place and she would find him another. Racing over to his bedroom, he hurried inside and stopped in his tracks. The room was empty and the window to the fire escape was wide open.

Chapter Twenty-Nine

This is do or die time for me.

Three weeks later, Logan watched how Dymond picked at her slice of pecan pie. She had told Joy that she didn't mind if he came over for Thanksgiving dessert, but it was a lie. Dymond hated he was here. However, something was going on deeper with her. He just couldn't figure out what it was. He wasn't going to find out anything unless he talked to her.

"Dymond, Joy told me this is your last year of college. Are you excited about that?"

"I guess," she answered without looking at him.

Okay, time for the next question, he thought peeking at Joy from the corner of his eyes. She looked a little nervous, but didn't say anything.

"What is your major?"

"Business Administration and computers with a minor in Journalism," came the same monotone reply.

"Sounds like you have a full schedule. You must be pretty smart to handle that plus a full-time job."

"I guess I am," Dymond replied finally looking at him. "Since you are asking a lot of questions, can I ask you some?"

"Dymond, this is the time or place," Joy interrupted. "We were having a good time. How about we try not to ruin it?"

"No, it's fine," Logan retorted. "I don't mind answering Dymond's questions." Maybe he would finally find out why she disliked him so much and hopefully he could fix it.

"Are you really in love with my sister?" Dymond asked, firing off her first question.

"Yes, I'm in love with Joy. She's the best thing that has *ever* happened to me. I don't know what I would do without her."

"Is that true or are you just saying it?"

"It's true. I'm in love with your sister. I hope that we'll be together for a long time."

"I don't believe you," Dymond countered.

"Why not?"

"My father told my mother that he was in love with her, too, but he really wasn't. If he had been, then he wouldn't have left us before I was born. Do you know what that did to my mother? She used to cry all the time in her bedroom. She didn't think I heard her, but I did. I never could do anything to make her feel better. After awhile, I think the grief of losing my father took her away."

Logan was taken aback. Joy never told him about this. She said her mother died, but she never really said it was from a broken heart. He didn't know what to say to Dymond. She was actually thinking he had plans to leave Joy in the future. That was so far from the truth, but she wasn't going to believe him if he said that to her now.

"Dymond, you have it wrong. Our mother was very happy raising us. She didn't die from a broken heart," Joy said, breaking into the conversation. There wasn't any kind of proof that their mother died from that, so she didn't want Dymond to keep thinking it.

"Yes, she did," Dymond shouted. "I won't let Logan do to you what my father did to our mother. He'll be here for a while and leave after he's done with you. You won't be able to handle the pain, and you'll die just like our mother did. I have to protect you from him," Dymond screamed. Jumping up from the table, she ran from the room.

"Did you know she felt like that?" Logan asked, still shocked by Dymond's outburst.

"No, I never knew that Dymond harbored that kind of resentment toward her father. We always tried to make the memory of Bill something special for her. He fell in love with her the second he knew about her. I guess I didn't do a good enough job."

"Brown eyes, don't fault yourself," Logan said. "Your mother dying when Dymond was so young was a traumatic experience. She had to blame someone and she picked her father despite the fact he had nothing to do with it. I think I need to leave so you can talk to her."

Logan got up from the table and waved Joy back down when she tried to stand up. "No, I can see myself out. How about you sit there and get your thoughts together. Your sister needs you right now. I'll call you in a couple of days to see how things are going. I think you need to spend this time with her." Walking around the table, he gave Joy a quick kiss on the mouth and left.

Chapter Thirty

Joy knocked on the door once and went inside her sister's room. She saw Dymond sitting on the ledge by her window. She was heartbroken that her little sister had been keeping her feelings bottled up for so long. It was past time they got things out in the open.

"Dymond, we need to talk about what happen with Logan."

"I know you're pissed that I went off on him like that. I'll go and apologize to him, but I only said what I thought," Dymond said looking away from the window at her.

"Honey, I'm not worried about what you said to Logan. He's a grown man and he can handle it. I'm more concerned about you. Do you really think that Mama cried all the time because of Bill?"

"Yes, I do. She never seemed really happy having me around."

"Why didn't you tell me this sooner?" Joy asked, taking a seat next to Dymond. "I never knew you felt like this."

"How could I tell you? You sent me off to that girl's school because I was getting on your nerves. You didn't want me around either."

Shaking her head, Joy placed her hand on top of Dymond's. "I never sent you to *Criswell* because I didn't want you around. I sent you there for an excellent education. I was keeping my promise to Mama. She

150

wanted us to have the best and I was trying to give it to you."

"Really?"

"Yes, really," she answered. "You're my baby sister and I was looking out for your best interest."

Dymond removed her hand from underneath hers and placed it in her lap. "Are you really in love with Logan?"

"Yes, I am."

"Don't you think you fell in love awfully fast with him? You barely know anything about him."

"I know everything I need to know. I'm not saying we're going to get married anytime soon, but he does make me happy," Joy answered. "It feels good to have someone to talk to after a long day of work about your problems."

"What if he leaves you? How will you handle it?"

"I won't die because we broke up. I might be upset for a little while, but I'll get over it. In addition, I want you to understand something, Dymond. Bill didn't leave you. He was killed during a shootout at a grocery store. He loved us and was going to marry our mother. Yes, she was upset by his death, but that isn't what eventually killed her. She just died."

"But she cried all the time. I heard her as a little girl and I was so upset by it."

"I think Mama was crying for the dream she would never have. Bill was her true love and it hurt when he wasn't there anymore."

"Was it wrong for her to have a baby by a married man?"

"Dymond, you were made out of love, so it wasn't wrong," Joy replied. "However, I do want to ask you something."

"What is it?"

"Why have you waited so long to let me know what you have been thinking? We could have had this discussion years ago."

"Every time I tried to bring it up, I couldn't. Plus, I didn't want you to think I was being immature, still harping on something from the past. I couldn't blame Mama, so I tossed the blame on Bill instead."

"I wish you had talked to me sooner, but now that you have, I'm going to make sure I spend more time with you so we can get things out in the open."

"What about Logan?" Dymond frowned. "Are you going to break up with him? I know he probably thinks I'm a bitch for saying that stuff to him."

"I think Logan has thicker skin than you think."

"Are you sure? I don't want to mess things up for you. He really isn't that bad."

Joy was thrilled that Dymond was coming to accept Logan. It seemed like things might be looking on the bright side after all.

Chapter Thirty-One

"What are you going to be doing today after your last class?" Joy asked Dymond who was sitting across from her at the table.

"I don't have to work, so I was just going to come home and watch some television. Why?"

"I was wondering; do you want to get some early Christmas shopping done with me? I'm going to be working a lot of shifts at the hospital for the next couple of weeks. The holidays are coming up, and it's always the worst time at work."

"I would love that. There are a couple of things I saw on sale that I would love to get. Have you decided what you're going to get for Logan? He hasn't been around in a couple of weeks. Are things going good with the two of you?"

"Everything is perfect. He called me last night while you were at work. He is just busy working on this case. Logan is still looking for the guy who shot him. I can't believe the cops haven't found him by now. Who would hide someone like that?" Joy exclaimed.

"I don't know. It's kind of scary knowing someone like that is out there walking the streets. Hey, I have an idea for you," Dymond said.

"What is it?"

"After we're finished shopping, why don't you invite Logan over for a while. I hate that the two of you are walking on eggshells because of me. I'm getting better with the two of you dating now. I'm beginning to see how

153

childish   I   was   being."
"Dymond, I wanted us to spend this time together," Joy insisted. She would love to spend some romantic time with Logan.

"Stop lying to me," Dymond laughed. "I saw the excitement come into your eyes. I need to take care of some personal stuff anyway. You'll have the house to yourself for several hours. Have fun and stop worrying about me so much. I've actually been thinking about finding my own place after I graduate."

"You don't have to move out. You can stay here as long as you want."

"Nope, I think I need to find my own place so I can handle my personal life."

Joy wondered if that personal life involved Ridge. She still wasn't fond of her sister hanging around that guy. There just wasn't something right about him. "Are you still friends with Ridge?"

Sighing, Dymond closed up her books and shoved them into her backpack on the floor. "I'm not getting into that with you. I'll see you at the mall around four o'clock. I'll be waiting for you on the inside." Getting up, she slipped the backpack on and grabbed her purse off the floor.

"Dymond, wait!" Joy yelled going after her sister. But she was too late. Her sister was already out the door.

No, she wasn't going to let that relationship continue. She was going to find out where Ridge lived and have a talk with him. He needed to know that she didn't trust him and would do anything to protect her sister from him.

Chapter Thirty-Two

"God, baby, I have missed being here with you like this. It seems like forever since we have made love. Thank God you called me. I was about to break down and beg to come over here. Do you know how hard it was being away from you this long?" Logan mumbled against her neck before raining kisses down it.

"I know. I have missed the hell out of you, too, handsome. But you knew why. I had to spend these past weeks with my sister, and it has paid off. She's doing a lot better, which means we can spend more time together."

"More time like this?" Logan asked cupping her breast in his hand. He ran his thumb over her nipple, causing her to moan.

"Yeah, I think more time like this is very good."

"Wonderful. How about you pack a bag after we are finished, and you can spend the weekend at my home. I have enough food there to last us the weekend. We can make up for lost time."

"Mmmm… I love the sound of that. Are you sure you can handle all of these extracurricular activities? I have a lot of pent-up energy I want to work off. Work has really been hard the last couple of days."

"I have something hard that needs your special attention," Logan growled, easing his thick cock inside her body. "Can you feel it?"

Licking her lips, Joy wrapped her legs around Logan's waist, pulling him deeper into her body. It felt wonderful to be so full of him again. "Yeah, I think I can handle all of this and more."

"Glad to hear it."

The slow thrust of Logan's hips brought a smile to Joy's face. The few boyfriends she had in the past didn't know how to love her like this. Sometimes Logan wanted it down and dirty and other times he wanted it slow and sweet. She never knew which one he was going to do. She loved to be kept guessing by him. Her orgasm hit her slowly, working its way through her body.

Biting down on Logan's shoulder, she rode the wave of ecstasy and heard Logan screaming his release a few seconds later before he fell on her. They stayed like that for a few minutes before Logan rolled off her and tugged her against his side.

"Honey, that was so good. I can't believe I went almost two weeks without making love to you. It was hard enough not being able to see you. We can't let that happen again. Are you listening to me?" Logan asked, running his fingertips over her ribs.

Laughing, Joy brushed Logan's hands off her and turned around to face him. The loving look in his eyes made her heart beat a little faster. "I agree with you. We need to spend more time with each other."

"I have an idea."

"What is it?" Joy asked, tracing Logan's bottom lip with her finger.

"Move in with me."

The suggestion caught her completely off guard. She couldn't move in with Logan. She couldn't abandon her sister like that. Why would Logan suggest such a thing?

"I can't move in with you. Where would Dymond go?"

"I was thinking maybe we could get some money together and help her make the rest of the payments on your house until she graduates and finds a job."

Joy couldn't believe this. Dymond was talking about moving out on her own earlier today, and now Logan comes up with this idea. Could her life really be this good? Dymond loved the house they lived in and she did have some extra money saved back for her sister as a graduation present. She couldn't say yes until she talked with Dymond about this. Things have been so much better between them, and she wasn't going to have a setback.

"I have to talk this over with Dymond."

"Does that mean you want to be my roommate?"

"Does your roommate get to go to bed and wake up with you every morning?"

"I wouldn't have it any other way," Logan replied, kissing her. "Do you think New Years would be too soon? I don't think I can wait until May to have you in my home."

"New Years?" Joy gasped. "We haven't even made it through Christmas yet. Can't we just take it one day at a time?'

"I don't need anything for Christmas if you are going to be my New Years present," Logan replied.

"How about you let me see what Dymond thinks about this, and I'll give you my answer at Christmas?"

"Christmas... That's two weeks away. I don't think I can wait that long."

Pushing Logan on his back, Joy climbed on top of him and nibbled at the corner of his mouth. "Come on. I know you can do this for me. Please?" she asked, softly.

"You know that I can't deny you anything when you do that to me," he growled.

"Does that mean yes?"

"Yes, I can wait until Christmas for your answer."

"What can I do to thank you for being such an understanding boyfriend?"

Turning his head, Logan whispered something into Joy's ear, making her gasp. "Are you sure we can use your handcuffs like that?"

"Positive," Logan answered and gave her a wickedly sexy wink.

Chapter Thirty-Three

The next day back at her house, Joy tried to keep the smile off her face at the excitement that lit up Dymond's gorgeous face. Her sister was thrilled at the news that she might be living in their house by herself after New Years. This was going way better than she could have guessed.

"Are you sure about this? You don't mind if I move in with Logan and leave you here? I can stay here until you graduate. Logan will understand."

"No," Dymond shouted and calmed down. "The two of you need your own space and I need mine. I think I have been dependent on you for way too many years. I'll be twenty-one in a couple of months and I need the responsibility. I have to prove I can do this. Besides, you spend more time at Logan's house than you do here. It only makes sense that you move in with him."

"Hey, I spend time here," Joy denied.

"Yeah, right. I haven't seen you since Friday. You are already practically living with the man in blue," Dymond laughed. "I can't wait until I get to move my stuff into the bigger bedroom. I love your walk-in closet. I have been hating on you about that since I moved back home."

"Are you serious?"

"I'm your sister. I wouldn't lie to you? Now since that is all settled, how about we go out for dinner tonight? There's this new Thai restaurant that I want to try out," Dymond suggested.

"I love Thai food."

"That's why I suggested it, so get your butt moving."

* * * *

"I don't see you in weeks and when I do, you pop this kind of news on me. Damn man, do you have anything else shocking to tell me?" Marcus' voice had a degree of warmth and a hint of concern.

Leaning back in his seat, Logan laughed at his friend's reaction. He truly didn't think it was that big of a deal. He was in love with Joy and asked her to move in with him. People in love move in together all the time. It was always the next step in any loving relationship.

"Besides that, I'm crazy in love with Joy," he said. "No, that's it for now. I think that is enough, don't you?"

"Yeah, I believe that it is," Marcus laughed. "Do you realize that you're going to break a certain woman's heart when she finds out this news?"

Logan knew who Marcus was talking about, but he wasn't about to say the name. Peggy hadn't approached him about them dating anymore, so he assumed that she had gotten over the idea all together. Now it seems that she hadn't after all.

"Are you referring to Peggy?"

"You guessed it. She was still holding out hope that you and she would be a couple."

"How do you know this? She hasn't said anything to me in weeks. We have been working on the leads that come in about Ridge and nothing else."

"She has been coming to me on the days you aren't here, asking how things are going with Joy. She really hates her, you know," Marcus told him.

"I wouldn't say that she hates Joy. She is just a little jealous."

"No, Peggy HATES her. Don't believe anything else. I'm telling you the truth."

"Great... I don't want Peggy giving me her opinion about this," Logan complained. "How can I deal with this without making it a difficult work environment around here?"

"What do you not want to tell me?" Peggy's voice asked behind them.

Spinning around, Logan and Marcus stared at Peggy not ten feet behind them giving them a hard look. She already seemed pissed and he hadn't even told her yet. He shouldn't care what Peggy thought, but he didn't want her bothering Joy. Without a doubt, Peggy would confront his woman about this. It was just the kind of person she was. That part of her personality made her an excellent cop, but it didn't work so well when it came to relationships.

"Good luck, Logan," Marcus said getting up. "You're going to need it." Logan watched as his friend disappeared around the corner, leaving him alone in the break room with Peggy.

"Sit down, Peggy, we need to talk." Logan pointed to the chair in front of him and silently prayed that this would go better than he hoped, but he knew it wouldn't.

Chapter Thirty-Four

After his disastrous conversation with Peggy, the next couple of weeks went by in a whirlwind for Logan. He split his holiday time between his family, work, and Joy. He still couldn't believe how fast New Years came and went. The only good thing about it was now Joy was living with him, and he was having the best time of his life. He also found out something else about his girlfriend. She loved the old railroad track by his house. It wasn't in use anymore, but for some reason, Joy found it sexy.

He always knew that something had been missing in his home, and now he knew what it was....*Joy*. She added a special quality to his life that had been missing before. He didn't mind getting out of bed anymore, because he had her to go home to. It was the best feeling in the world, and he had a hunch it was only going to get better.

However, he could really start his New Year off with a bang if he finally caught up with Ridge. All of the leads that came in ended up being dead ends, and it was starting to get on his nerves. Last week, he thought he might have had a bit of good luck when another officer picked up Luther for selling stolen guns two blocks from a high school, but Luther wasn't offering up any information. He didn't even care this was his third strike, and he was going to get some serious jail time. He wasn't turning on his partner. So now, he was back to square one and nothing to go on.

"I'm not giving up until I find Ridge," Logan mumbled to himself. "He's going to be locked up sooner than he thinks. I just need that one good lead, and I'll get him."

* * * *

"It's almost time for me to do the last of my plan. I got everything I need now to ruin their happy little world. I found out something that is going to make my retribution all the sweeter," the woman laughed, kneeling down at the grave. "I don't have that much time left, so I have to get it done soon. You would be so proud of me. I never forgot the stories you told me when I was a kid. You were so unhappy. I couldn't make you happy back then, but I can do it now."

"Do you know how many times I have looked into their faces, and they act like I don't even exist to them? Well, after I finish what I want to do, they won't ever forget my name. This town will have to give me the respect that I deserve, along with everything else they stole from us."

Chapter Thirty-Five

Thank God Dymond has come to her senses. I never thought it would happen.

"Give me the address, and I will go and do it, but you need to get him out of your life. You have grown past dating guys like him. I don't care about going and telling him to leave you the hell alone."

"Joy, I can do this. I can just skip class today and talk to Ridge. I won't let you get involved with this," Dymond retorted.

Standing in front of the bedroom door, Joy crossed her arms over her chest, blocking Dymond's only exit. She wasn't going to move until her sister did what she wanted. How could she be living with Logan now and have this Ridge character still hanging around? Just yesterday, she came by and found him in their house. It was a good thing Logan dropped her off instead of coming in. She might have told her boyfriend to toss Ridge out of here.

"I'm not budging on this. Give me the address so I can take care of this before I go to work for my paycheck."

"Fine," Dymond complained. She wrote the information down on a piece of paper and waved it under her nose.

"I hope Logan has seen this stubborn streak in you."

"He has and he loves me even more for it," Joy grinned, taking the paper. "I'll call you once I have taken care of this."

"I thought you were living with Logan now. Isn't he keeping you busy enough? What are you doing here?

"I gave him a special good-bye this morning before work." Joy winked. "So, yes, he is keeping me busy enough. Besides, what kind of sister would I be if I didn't drop by unannounced?"

"Oh, you are just so nasty. I don't want to hear about you getting some with your boyfriend."

"Hey, you asked and I told you," Joy answered, indulgently.

"Remind me next time not to ask."

"Fine. I can tell I have worn out my welcome. I'm leaving." Joy spun around on her heel and strode out the door.

"Joy, wait," Dymond yelled after her.

"What?" She looked back over her shoulder at her sister.

"Thanks for doing this for me."

"You're welcome." Joy waved good-bye and continued on her way.

Chapter Thirty-Six

Sitting outside in her car, Peggy stared at Joy's house wondering how she was going to make her rival understand that she wasn't the right woman for Logan. Logan was just being blindsided by the newness of being with Joy. He wasn't really in love with her. She couldn't let them move in together. It just wasn't going to happen, and she would make sure she put a stop to it.

She was about to open the door and get out when Joy came out of the house and walked down the snow-covered sidewalk and got into her car. "Where in the hell is she going? I need to talk to her." Peggy started her car and followed behind Joy.

It seemed like she drove close to an hour before Joy finally pulled into a rundown motel at the outskirts of town. Peggy stayed in her car as she watched Joy get out, look around the place, and stop in front of a motel room door at the end of the building.

"Who does she know in a place like this? I wouldn't think the perfect little nurse would set foot on property like this," she mumbled to herself. Could she be cheating on Logan? This could be the thing she needed to get Logan over his blind love for Joy. Leaning across the steering wheel, she tried to get a better look at the motel room number, but it was too far away. She watched as Joy knocked a couple more times before she moved away.

As Joy was heading to her car, Peggy noticed an expensive black car speeding around the corner of the building heading directly for Joy. She thought the car was going to stop, but watched in horror mingled with a huge amount of excitement as the car hit Joy and kept going.

"Who in the hell was that?" Peggy yelled, looking out her window in the direction the vehicle disappeared. Dragging her attention back to Joy, she looked at her lifeless body lying in the snow. She should get out of the car and help her, but she wouldn't. She secretly hoped that Joy was dead. Logan didn't need her in his life. She hadn't been nothing but a pain in her side since the first day she meet her.

Only a few minutes past before a man came rushing out of the manager's office to check on the noise and saw Joy on the ground. Peggy cursed under her breath as he ran over to Joy's body and checked her for any signs of life.

She watched in disappointment as he pulled a cell phone out of his jacket pocket and dialed a number. She could only assume it was the police and an ambulance. She knew that she shouldn't be here when they showed up. She couldn't afford anyone recognizing her car.

Peggy gave Joy one final look, hoping that the person who hit Joy had taken care of her problem before she drove off and headed back for the police station.

* * * *

The feel of her cell phone vibrating inside her jacket pocket drew Dymond's attention away from the professor's lecture. She knew it was probably Joy calling her to tell her how things went with Ridge. She didn't have enough nerve to tell him things were over, but she shouldn't have sent her sister to do it for her.

She glanced at the caller ID on her phone frowning at the unfamiliar number. "Who in the world is this?" she mumbled to herself before answering the call.

"Hello?"

"Is this Dymond Simmons?" a strange male voice asked.

"Yes, I'm her. How may I help you?"

"Are you related to Joy Simmons?"

Dymond felt her heart catch in the middle of her chest. This couldn't be good news at all. What was wrong with her sister? She was almost too scared to even voice her next question. She knew Ridge's voice and this guy on the phone wasn't him.

"I'm her sister. What's wrong?"

"Joy was hit by a car. We need you to get to the hospital ASAP. She's unconscious and the doctors are about to take her into surgery. We need someone to sign her paperwork. Are you eighteen?"

Her sister was hit by a car and needed surgery. What in the hell happened when Joy went to see Ridge? Was he the one that ran her over? Dymond couldn't think from the pounding going on in her head. She had to get to the hospital as fast as she could and see about Joy. She couldn't die. She wouldn't have anyone else left in the world.

"Ma'am, are you still there?" The guy asked her.

"I'm here. I'm twenty, so I can sign the paperwork. I'll be there in twenty minutes, if not sooner." Dymond ended the call and threw her phone inside her purse. She quickly gathered up all her stuff and raced out of the classroom.

* * * *

In less than twenty minutes, Dymond made it to the hospital and signed the papers that were waiting for her at the front desk. She couldn't believe this was happening to her. She knew Joy got hurt going to see Ridge. He didn't live in the best part of town and now her sister may die because of her. If Joy didn't make it, she wouldn't be able to forgive herself. She was the one who brought Ridge into their lives. She should have never started a relationship with him out of spite. Now her being a major bitch was coming back to haunt her.

God, why did she have to be such an idiot and keep hanging out with Ridge? She knew he wasn't the type of guy Joy wanted her around. But that bad boy side of him kept calling to her, and now Joy was in surgery for her bad judgment and may not make it. No, she wasn't going to think the worst. Joy was going to be okay, and she was going to make this up to her sister anyway she could.

Dropping her head into her hands, Dymond tried to blink back her sudden tears so she could be strong for Joy. However, they started to pour from her eyes anyway. It seemed like they were going to last forever. She was so caught up in her own turmoil that she almost didn't hear the man yelling at the nurse's station.

"I know that she's here. Tell me what is going on with her. I don't care if I'm not family. I'm her boyfriend and I have a damn right to know what is going on!"

Raising her head, Dymond brushed the rest of the tears away from her eyes and stared at Logan. She was stunned to see him here. She thought Joy had mentioned in passing Logan was busy talking to people on the streets about a difficult case.

"Logan, over here," she yelled, drawing his attention.

"What in the hell is going on?" he demanded, taking a seat across from her.

"I thought you were out working a case about your shooting."

"I was and Marcus called me on my cell phone. He heard about Joy getting hit by a car. How is she doing? Have the police caught the driver?"

Dymond shook her head. "No, I don't think so. Joy is in surgery. The doctors think she has a lot of internal injuries. I can't lose my sister. She's the only person I have left in the world. I should have never sent her to that motel to talk to him. I'm the reason she got hit by that car."

"Motel? What was Joy doing at a motel?"

"I was having problems getting rid of a guy and Joy went to talk to him. She got hit there. I should never have let her go. It was my problem, not hers."

"Don't blame yourself. Joy wouldn't blame you. She's very protective of you and would have gone if you hadn't asked her to. Right now, we need to focus on good thoughts so Joy can come out of this surgery with flying colors."

"You're right," Dymond agreed as Logan moved next to her and wrapped his arm around her shoulder.

Four hours passed as Dymond and Logan sat in the sterile waiting room praying the doctor would be out soon to tell them how Joy was doing. As Dymond was about to give up hope of anything happening, the doctor came through the door and paused in front of them.

"How is Joy doing?" Logan asked, beating her to the question.

"She had less internal injuries than we thought, so that was good. Nothing on her spine was broken. However, she does have a broken leg in two places. It's going to take a while for that to heal. In addition, there was some scrapes by the side of her head, but no swelling on the brain."

"That's wonderful," Dymond said cutting in.

"She's going to need physical therapy for her leg and she might be in pain for a while."

"Do you think the accident will leave her with a limp?" Logan inquired.

"I don't think so. It's all about how the bone heals and how well she adjusts to her physical therapy," the doctor answered.

"Can we go and see her?" Dymond asked.

"I usually only recommend one person at a time. But since there are only two of you, it should be okay. She might still be out of it a little. When I left recovery, she was starting to wake up. By now she should be in ICU."

"Thank you, doctor, for saving Joy. I love her so much. I wouldn't know what I would do without her." Logan stood up and offered the doctor his hand.

"It was my pleasure." The doctor shook his hand, nodded his head at Dymond and left.

"Come on," Dymond said, grabbing him by the arm dragging him in the direction of ICU. "I want to see how Joy is doing with my own eyes."

* * * *

Walking into the hospital room behind Dymond, Logan bit back a curse at the sight of Joy's left leg bandaged up and propped up on several pillows. The white gauze stood out against her beautiful dark skin. He had never felt such rage in his life. He wanted to kill the bastard who did this to his woman. She looked so small lying there. This isn't the strong woman he loved and was used to seeing.

"Brown eyes, how are you feeling?" He stood on the side of the bed that Dymond wasn't at.

Opening her eyes, Joy gave him a small smile. "I'm in a little pain," her voice croaked. "What happened to me?"

"You don't remember?"

Joy shook her head.

"You were hit by a car outside a motel," he told her.

"It's all my fault," Dymond cried, interrupting their conversation. "You went to see him because of me. I could have gotten you killed."

"Dymond, stop crying," Joy whispered softly. "I don't blame you."

"I can't help it. I hate seeing you like this. I need to go and get some air." Dymond glanced at Logan. "Can you stay here with her until I get back later?" She couldn't really let Joy or Logan know where she really was going.

He wasn't about to leave Joy's side. She was going to have a permanent shadow, and it was going to be him. "I'm staying for a while. Where are you going?"

"Home. I need to get something for Joy. I'll be back soon." Leaning over the bed, Dymond kissed Joy and moved back. "I won't be gone long." She practically ran from the room.

Logan thought Dymond should stay, but he could tell she was more upset than she was letting on. He hoped Dymond wasn't gone too long, because he didn't think this hit and run was by accident. Someone wanted to hurt Joy and he wasn't sure if Dymond was the next person on their list.

Chapter Thirty-Seven

Outside in the parking lot, Dymond tried unlocking her car a couple of times before she finally got the key to work. She got inside, tossing her purse and book bag onto the passenger seat. She started the car and was about to drive off when she looked in the rearview mirror and saw Ridge sitting in her back seat. She didn't have time to scream before she felt the knife against her neck.

"Ridge, what are you doing?" she gasped. Joy was right. Ridge was out of his mind. He had tried to kill Joy and now she was next on his list.

"Dymond, I need you to listen carefully. I don't want to hurt you, but I will. Do you understand me?"

"Tell me what's going on."

Instead of answering her, Ridge pressed the knife harder against her neck. She felt the sting of the blade and a drop of blood going down her neck. "Stop questioning me and just do as I say. Do you get it?"

Dymond nodded her head. "I get it."

"Do you know where that old house is out on Highway 286? A lot of the college kids have parties out there at night."

"Yes, I know where it is."

"Good. Start your car and drive there. Don't ask me any questions on the way. I don't usually kill a person with a knife, so don't become my first victim."

Without saying a word, Dymond pulled out of the hospital parking lot and drove in the direction that Ridge wanted. All the way there, all she could think about was how her restlessness got her into this mess in the first place.

Once they got to their destination, Ridge told her to pull around back and get out of the car. After she got out, for a split second she thought about running and then decided against it. She didn't want Ridge to kill her. Without a doubt now, she knew he was the person who ran over her sister.

"Why did you hit my sister? What did she ever do to you?"

"I didn't hit that nosy bitch sister of yours," Ridge shouted behind her. "Now go inside the house and stop asking so many fucking questions."

She wasn't about to take another step until she got some answers. Ridge said he wasn't the person who hit Joy. However, he didn't say that he didn't know who the person was.

"Move!" He poked her in the middle of the back with the knife. She winced at the pain, but stood her ground.

"I'm not moving until you tell me who hit my sister."

"If you get your ass moving, you'll find out who it was." Ridge shoved her hard in the shoulder, forcing her to move toward the back door of the house. Inside he kept pushing her until she went up the back steps and down a long hallway.

"What's going on?"

"Shut up and open the door."

Dymond pushed open the door and froze as her eyes connected with Haley.

"Haley, why in the fuck are you here?"

"Welcome home, little sister," Haley laughed, yanking her completely into the room by the arm.

* * * *

Logan glanced at his watch for the fifth time since Dymond left over three hours ago. There was no way she was still at the house. Where in the hell could she be? Joy was asleep now, but as soon as she woke up, she would be asking about her sister. Something wasn't right here. What was going on that he didn't know about?

Taking one last look at Joy, he got up from his seat and went into the hallway. Maybe if he stayed here a few minutes, he would see Dymond coming back. If not, he would call an officer to stay with Joy while he went looking for Dymond. He hoped she didn't go looking for that boyfriend she was having problems with. She was adamant that he was the reason Joy got hit in the first place.

"Logan," a male voice yelled at him.

He frowned at the sight of Marcus hurrying toward him. "What are you doing here?"

Marcus stopped in front of him. "We found Ridge."

"What? Where? How?"

"A guy that delivers the newspapers saw Ridge dragging a girl into the old Richardson's place."

"How are you sure that it's him? We have had a lot of bad leads over the last couple of months. I can't believe this until we have proof."

"It's true," Marcus said. "We finally got Luther to turn on him. Luther said the house belonged to the parents of a girl Ridge was dating, but there is more."

Logan wasn't getting a good feeling about the 'more' part. "What? I never heard about Ridge having a girlfriend. Who in the hell would be crazy enough to date him?"

"Luther also told us that Ridge had been seeing another girl on the side."

For some reason, he was afraid to ask. "Who is the other girl?"

"Joy's sister, Dymond."

"Damn it!" he yelled. "I need to get out there. Where's Peggy? She has been working this case with me. She would want to be in on this."

"I don't know. No one can find her."

Logan knew he didn't have any time to waste. Dymond was in trouble, and he had to get to her before Ridge killed her. "Can you stay here with Joy? Don't let her know about any of this."

"Sure, I can stay. What do you want me to tell her if she asks about you and Dymond?"

"I don't know. Just think of something, but don't tell her the truth," Logan hollered back as he raced towards the stairway.

* * * *

"You aren't my sister!" Dymond screamed at Haley, jerking her arm out of the tight grip. "I only have one sister, and she is at the hospital right now. What kind of game are you trying to pull with Ridge?"

"You are such an idiot," Haley said, walking in a circle around her body. "I'm not talking about us having the same mother. Bill Richardson was my dad, too, and should have been home with me and my mother. Instead, he was with Danielle and it got him killed."

"You're lying," Dymond gasped, taking a step back, running into Ridge who shoved her away from him. "If I had another sister, Joy would have told me."

"No one knew my mother was pregnant but her and my dad. She told me how your mother would sleep with my father in their bed. Danielle Simmons was a slut! I wish she was still alive. I could have run her over with my car instead of your bitch of a sister."

"You hit Joy!" Dymond lunged for Haley only to be pulled back by Ridge. She struggled to get out of his grip, but he wasn't letting her go.

"It's so hot watching the two of you fight. I can see the family resemblance now."

"Ridge, shut the fuck up!" Haley shouted. "I look nothing like this tramp. Her family is the reason my mother killed herself when I was thirteen. I got shipped off to foster care until I was eighteen. The hate I have for you burned in my heart all of those years. I promised my mother everyday at her grave I was going to get you back."

"Haley, we are sisters. You don't want to hurt me," Dymond said, trying to reason with the distraught woman in front of her.

"We aren't sisters. You are just the mistake my father made that I'm going to fix. Let her go Ridge and leave us alone."

Dymond knew this might the only chance she had to escape. The second Ridge let her arm go, she dug her high heel into his foot and ran around his body. She raced back down the stairs Ridge shoved her up earlier. Halfway down, she ran into Logan and several officers coming up the stairs.

"Dymond, are you okay?" he asked.

"Yes, but they are still upstairs. Haley ran over Joy. She wanted to kill both of us."

"We know everything," Logan said, handing her over to another officer behind him. "Take her to the car and wait for me."

The sounds of footsteps running toward them got closer and closer. Dymond stepped behind the officer, terrified of what was going to happen. She saw Ridge run around the corner first with the knife in his hand and Haley was close behind him.

"Drop the weapon or I'll shoot," Logan said, pointing his gun directly at Ridge.

"I'm not going to jail," Ridge screamed before he charged at Logan. One shot rang out, and Ridge fell dead on the middle of the stairs. Haley tried to spin around and head back upstairs, but Logan's voice stopped her.

"Miss Richardson, unless you want to end up like your boyfriend, I suggest you get down on your knees and fold you hands behind your head."

"I want that bitch dead," Haley screamed, twirling and pointing a finger at her. "Her family is the reason my mother is dead. I have to make her pay."

"Miss Richardson, don't make me ask you again," Logan shouted. "This is your last warning."

Dymond watched as Haley did as she was told, and officers rushed to cuff her. "I can't believe she's my sister and wanted to kill me," she whispered.

"Haley is a very sick young woman. She has been in and out of mental institutions for years," Logan told her as he led her down the stairs and out to his car. "She just escaped from the last one she was in and made her way here. Come on. Let's get to the hospital so we can check on Joy."

"Does she know what happened?" This was so much for her to process. She didn't know how in the world Joy was going to be able to do it.

"No. When I left, she was with Marcus. He promised not to tell her anything," Logan told her as he helped her inside the car before getting in on the driver's side.

* * * *

The figure slowly entered Joy's room and didn't spare a second glance at Marcus asleep a few feet away from the bed. They only had one goal in mind, and that was getting rid of Joy for good. Why couldn't the hit and run driver taken care of this for her? It would have worked out so much better that away.

Picking up a pillow off the bed, Peggy hid the gun inside of it and eased closer to a sleeping Joy. What was so damn perfect about her that Logan wanted her to live with him? He was hers and had been since she saw him at the water foundation the first day she got assigned to the station. Well, it wouldn't matter in a few minutes. Joy would be dead, and Logan would be all hers. Raising the gun, she aimed for Joy.

"Peggy, drop the gun," Marcus yelled at her.

Glancing up, Peggy tried to fire at Marcus but was too slow. She staggered back from his bullet hitting her in the upper part of the chest. She flew against the wall and crumbled to the floor. The last thought on her mind was Logan before she died.

Marcus walked over to Peggy's body to make sure she was dead and turned his attention to Joy. She was sitting up in the bed with a wide-eyed look on her face as doctors and nurses ran into the room.

"This lady was trying to kill this patient. I had to shoot her. Please find something to cover up the body. This is a crime scene." Marcus quickly made a phone call to Logan and then went to check on Joy, because she looked to be in shock.

Chapter Thirty–Eight

Ten minutes after Marcus' phone call, Logan rushed into Joy's room and freaked out at all the blood covering the wall and the bed. His eyes searched around the room, but he didn't see Joy anywhere in sight.

"Where in the hell is Joy?" he hollered inside the crowded room. Several people stopped working and looked at him, but no one said a word. "Someone better answer me or I'm about to go off."

"Logan, calm down. Joy is fine," Marcus said coming towards him from across the room. "The doctors moved her to a different room so we can have this one."

"Were you telling me the truth over the phone? Peggy came in here and tried to kill her?"

"Yes. Peggy thought I was asleep. She grabbed a pillow off the end of the bed, slipped her gun inside and aimed for Joy. I yelled for her to stop. She didn't, and I had to shoot her." Marcus pointed to the covered up body by the wall.

"Are you positive that Joy is okay?"

"She's a little shaken up, but she'll be okay. Let me take you to her." Logan followed Marcus out of the room and down the hallway. "Where is Dymond?"

"She getting a cut on her neck looked it. She has been through a lot herself tonight. I hope both of them can come back from all of this," Logan commented.

"They both seem like very strong women to me. I'm sure that they will be fine after all of the shock wears off." Marcus stopped by a closed door. "She's in here. Take all the time you want. If Dymond comes looking for you, I'll point her in the right direction." Marcus touched him on the shoulder and left.

Opening the door, Logan walked into the room and found Joy sitting up in the bed staring out the window. He closed the door behind him and made his way over to her. He couldn't believe a couple of days ago he was secretly planning what to do for Valentine's Day and all of this happened. He would have lost her if Marcus hadn't been in the room. Just the thought sent a cold chill down his body.

"Joy?" he whispered, softly.

Joy's head turned away from the window, and she held her arms open for him. He raced over to the bed and gathered her up as close as he could with her leg. "Baby, I'm so sorry I wasn't here to protect you."

"What happened to you? Where's Dymond?" she asked, leaning back from him.

"It's a long story. I don't want to get into it now. I just want you to get better so I can drive you back across the railroad tracks you love so much by my house, and we can start planning our future together.

Epilogue

"Happy Valentine's Day baby!" Logan yelled as he came inside the den carrying a huge cake in his hand.

Tossing the romance book to the side, Joy slid up more on the couch and wondered what else her husband had done for her. The room was already filled with pink and white balloons. He had given her a gorgeous heart necklace and matching ring.

"What have you done?" she asked as Logan placed the cake down on the table in front of her.

"Take a look and let me know what you think. I had it ordered special at the bakery across town to celebrate our first Valentine's Day as a married couple."

Joy's eyes started to tear up as she looked at the cake. On the top was an interracial couple. The man was dressed like a cop and the woman was dressed like a nurse. They were holding hands as they stood in front of a railroad track. It was almost too beautiful for words.

"Logan, I love it. You shouldn't have gone through all of that trouble."

"It wasn't any trouble because I love you. You are everything I have been looking for in a woman and wife. I love you more than anything else in this world. I hope I can show you how much you mean to me each and every day we're married."

"I know you love me," Joy said, touching the side of Logan's face.

"How do you know that?" Logan asked turning his head to kiss the side of her palm.

"Because you made me Mrs. Logan Scott," she answered. "I couldn't ask for a better Valentine's Day present than that."

About the Author

Marie Rochelle is an award-winning author of erotic, interracial romance, including the Phaze titles *All the Fixin'*, *My Deepest Love: Zack*, and *Caught*. Visit her online at http://www.freewebs.com/irwriter/.

PHAZE SUPPORTS
EROTIC ALTRUISM

LOVE IS COLORBLIND

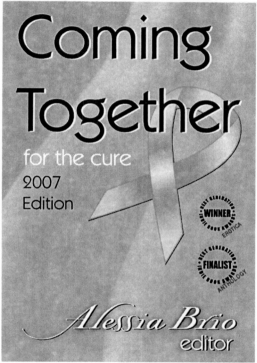

Coming Together

for the cure

2007
Edition

WINNER
EROTICA

FINALIST
ANTHOLOGY

Alessia Brio
editor

LaVergne, TN USA
24 September 2009
158932LV00001B/15/P